Received On

MAR – – 2019

Magnolia Library

THE MOST MARVELOUS INTERNATIONAL SPELLING BEE

Also by Deborah Abela

The Stupendously Spectacular Spelling Bee

The most marvelous INTERNATIONAL Spelling Bee

DEBORAH ABELA

sourcebooks
jabberwocky

First published in the United States in 2019 by Sourcebooks, Inc.

Copyright © 2018 by Deborah Abela
Cover and internal design © 2019 by Sourcebooks, Inc.
Cover design by Aleksei Bitskoff
Cover and internal illustrations by Aleksei Bitskoff

Sourcebooks and the colophon are registered trademarks of Sourcebooks, Inc.

Published by Sourcebooks Jabberwocky, an imprint of Sourcebooks, Inc.
P.O. Box 4410, Naperville, Illinois 60567-4410
(630) 961-3900
Fax: (630) 961-2168
sourcebooks.com

Originally published as *The Most Marvellous Spelling Bee Mystery* in 2018 in Australia by Penguin Random House Australia Pty Ltd, an imprint of Penguin Random House.

Library of Congress Cataloging-in-Publication Data

Names: Abela, Deborah, 1966- author.
Title: The Most Marvelous International Spelling Bee / Deborah Abela.
Description: Naperville, Illinois : Sourcebooks Jabberwocky, [2019] | Series:
  The Spectacular Spelling Bee ; book 2 | Originally published: Australia :
  Penguin Random House Australia, 2018. | Summary: India and her family
  travel to London, England for an international spelling bee, where she
  reconnects with friends, meets the queen, and investigates mysterious
  goings-on.
Identifiers: LCCN 2018038146 | (hardcover : alk. paper)
Subjects: | CYAC: Spelling bees--Fiction. | Family life--Fiction. |
  Self-confidence--Fiction. | Friendship--Fiction. | London
  (England)--Fiction. | England--Fiction. | Mystery and detective stories.
Classification: LCC PZ7.A15937 Mos 2019 | DDC [Fic]--dc23 LC record available at
https://lccn.loc.gov/2018038146

Source of Production: The Maple Press Company, York, Pennsylvania, United States.
Date of Production: January 2019
Run Number: 5013949

Printed and bound in the United States of America.
MA 10 9 8 7 6 5 4 3 2 1

Thank you to Hannah Mae, who was one of India's first fans, and to Mia and Emma, who insisted I write this book.

TRIUMPHANT

(adjective):

Victorious, successful,
and gloriously undefeated.

The town celebrated the champion's
triumphant return.

INDIA WIMPLE COULD SPELL. BRILLIANTLY. So brilliantly, in fact, that her family and country town of Yungabilla decided she would be the perfect candidate for the Stupendously Spectacular Spelling Bee.

Trouble was, India didn't agree.

For those of you who've met the Wimples, you know they're a family who never gives up—especially when it comes to each other. So with a clever plan and some colorful animal onesies, they convinced India to enter the bee. With Mom, Dad, Nanna Flo, and her brother, Boo, by her side, India made it all the way to the Sydney Opera House for the grand final…and won!

That was some feat for a young girl from a small town who was so nervous at even the *thought* of standing in front of strangers that she would often freeze on the spot.

This wasn't because India was unsure how to spell—she was always sure of that. It was mostly because of something that had happened to her when she was young—something frightening, sad, and even a little humiliating—that left her terribly anxious.

After India's triumphant win, her life was a whirlwind of interviews and photo shoots, but now that she was home, she hoped to get her old life back: the one with quiet afternoons lying beside Boo in their backyard while Mom told stories, or sitting in Gracie's Café sipping vanilla milkshakes, or reading on her bed for hours with no one paying her any attention at all.

But Mayor Bob had other ideas.

Which is why we start our story during a party on Main Street, with cake stalls, fresh juice stands, a sizzling barbecue, and the whole town seated in rows facing a podium with a banner made by Yungabilla Elementary School that read:

WELCOME HOME, INDIA WIMPLE
AUSTRALIA'S SPELLING CHAMPION!

The gymnastics team had just performed a series of shaky somersaults before their human pyramid collapsed under swooping magpies, and now the town was enjoying the school band, which was playing an unrecognizable tune where no one could hit a single note correctly or even play the wrong notes at the same time.

When the trombone player nudged the trumpeter in the back of the head, causing her to almost fall off the podium, the band stopped abruptly and scrambled back to their seats to rousing applause. It may not have been the best school band, but it was *Yungabilla's* school band, and that was something to cheer about.

Mayor Bob led the applause, his generous cheeks filling like balloons as he smiled. "Thank you for that fine rendition of—" He realized he had no idea *what* it was. "—that classic tune. And now, to the reason we are gathered here today. It gives me great pleasure to invite Yungabilla's newest hero and champion speller, India Wimple, to the stage."

India clenched her fist, crumpling the speech she'd prepared, while the audience hooted and clapped.

Even though she'd learned to manage her nerves during the spelling bee, the idea of standing in front of her entire town sent shivers right down to her toes. She silently hoped she wouldn't trip or faint.

Oh no. India hadn't thought of that. *What if I faint?*

Luckily, that was when Dad leaned over.

He took the balled-up speech and smoothed it out. "We'll be right here if you need us."

Nanna Flo, Mom, and Boo all nodded.

And just like that, India felt better. Simply being with her family made her feel braver, and even though she was still a little scared, she stepped up to the podium to excited applause and whistles.

"Go, India!" shouted Daryl, Dad's best friend.

"India Wimple," Mayor Bob said, "as a token of our tremendous admiration, I present you with a plastic replica of the town's largest zucchini and…the Yungabilla Medallion." He placed the ribbon and medal around India's neck. "This medallion is awarded to our finest—like Mathilda Hide, who rescued a herd of cows from a muddy bog, and Daryl Proudman, who saved a busload of schoolkids from being swept into floodwaters. You showed those city slickers the Yungabilla spirit and made us very proud."

The crowd was on their feet again, this time led by the cries of Daryl and the Wimples.

India looked at the expectant faces of the townspeople, all of them smiling and eager to hear what she had to say.

She'd lived in Yungabilla all her life and knew nearly everyone. There was Gracie Hubbard from the café; Mrs. O'Donnell from the bakery, who made India's favorite blueberry cheese-cake; Joe Miller, the butcher; her teacher, Mrs. Wild; and all the kids from school. They were there just to see her.

You can do this, India Wimple.

This was the voice in India's head. When it first started, it often warned her that her greatest fears were about to come true, but after winning the bee, it had become her devoted fan.

"Dear Mayor," India read from her notes, "thank you for your kind words, and to everyone here for all the support you gave me during the Stupendously Spectacular Spelling Bee. Without you and my family, I'd never have been able to—"

India didn't say another word, because at that precise moment, Farmer Austin's prizewinning cow, Bessie, pulled away from her owner's normally strong grip and stampeded through the crowd.

"Bessie!"

People dove out of the way, sending chairs flying as Bessie zigzagged toward the podium, straight toward India.

"Oh no," she breathed.

Dad leaped onto the stage and swept her out of the way just as the cow barreled past, knocking over the microphone stand and tearing through the school's specially made banner.

"Bessie!" Austin sprinted after his cow, who at that moment

crashed into the refreshment stand, splashing juice onto everyone nearby. That's when Austin realized where she was headed.

"Watch out, Mrs. O'Donnell!"

For India's special ceremony, Mrs. O'Donnell had filled an entire table with her homemade scones, vanilla custard, and lamingtons—lamingtons which were now being flung into the air in a whirlwind of coconut and sponge cake as Bessie gleefully guzzled them down.

Austin finally managed to reach her. He offered her hay from his back pocket. "Sorry, everyone. She's normally very calm, but lamingtons drive her bananas."

India stared down Main Street from the safety of the podium.

Bessie had left quite a trail of destruction: upturned tables and a carpet of squashed cakes and scones.

Dad muttered to India, "Your speech needs to be good to top that."

As the townsfolk of Yungabilla staggered to their feet and wiped cream and cake from their clothes and faces, another surprising thing happened.

"India!" Mrs. Rahim from the post office raced toward them. Her head scarf and dress fluttered behind her, and she was waving something above her head. "My darling," she puffed. "There's a special delivery for you. All the way from England."

The crowd parted to let Mrs. Rahim through. When she reached the podium, she handed India a cream-colored envelope. It was addressed in swirling gold lettering and sealed with a red wax crest.

"I don't know what it is," Mrs. Rahim said as she tried to catch her breath, "but it seems important. I can feel it."

The whole town watched as India carefully broke the seal and slipped out the letter. She read it again and again, unable to believe it was real.

"What does it say?" Dad asked.

Everyone gathered closer as India read it aloud, being careful not to miss a single word.

Dear India Wimple,

As the Australian champion of the Stupendously Spectacular Spelling Bee, you are hereby invited to compete in the Most Marvelous International Spelling Bee in London, England. The top three spellers from each participating country will join us…

India couldn't go on, mostly because the town burst into raucous cheers and Bessie let out a loud *moo*. Dad, Mom, Nanna Flo, and Daryl climbed onto the stage and smothered India in hugs. Boo caught her eye through the tangle of arms and gave her a look that said, *That's my sister.*

Mayor Bob pulled the microphone from a puddle of orange juice and wiped it against his shirt. "Our very own India Wimple is going to represent our small town on the world stage." A blob of vanilla custard slid from his hair to his shoulder. "This is going to make Yungabilla a tourist destination not to be missed. Now we *really* need to celebrate!"

There was spontaneous singing and dancing, and the school band attempted another tune, although which tune it was remained a mystery.

As the town lined up to shake India's hand and wish her the

best, she kept thinking about something in the invitation that she hadn't mentioned. There was a small detail she knew would ruin the moment, which she couldn't do—not when everyone looked so happy, including Dad, who grabbed Mom and twirled her around while Nanna Flo, Boo, and Daryl clapped and cheered them on.

Yungabilla was in the middle of a drought that had devastated farms, closed businesses, and forced people to leave town and find work somewhere else. Their population had dwindled to only four hundred people. In the last few years, good news had been rare. India knew she'd soon have to tell them what else was in the letter, but for now, she tucked it into her pocket, and the party continued long into the night.

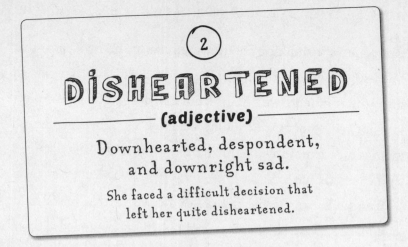

2

DISHEARTENED

(adjective)

Downhearted, despondent,
and downright sad.

She faced a difficult decision that
left her quite disheartened.

"MY DAUGHTER IS going to London!"

Dad was still excited by India's invitation and had been shouting the news all the way home, kicking up his heels and occasionally bursting into song. India loved seeing her dad so happy, even though the neighbors were probably not so happy about his voice.

"Why doesn't he have *any* of your singing talent?" Boo whispered to Nanna Flo, who back in the day was known to be quite the songstress.

"Beats me." Nanna pulled her hat over her ears. "I love your father, but I've heard cows in labor sound sweeter than him."

They snickered sneakily and continued walking in the moonlight.

When they reached home, Nanna Flo made a round of hot chocolates while Dad told stories of when he and Mom lived in

London as a young couple. He described all their favorite places and how this time, it was going to be even more special because the whole family would be there.

India knew it was time to tell Dad the truth.

"I have an announcement to make."

"Is it that I have the smartest daughter in the world?" Dad took a noisy sip of hot chocolate.

"Not quite," she said. "I'm not going to London."

Dad spat his drink all over the table. "What?"

"I've decided not to accept the invitation." India tried to sound determined, but she could hear her voice waver.

"I know competing in London is daunting," Mom said, "and it's natural to feel nervous, but you'll be magnificent."

"It's not nerves, Mom. It's this." India pulled the letter from her pocket and began to read:

> As an invited contestant, all expenses will be paid for
> you and one chaperone for the duration of the bee.

India slowly looked up. "There's no way we can all afford to be there, and I can't compete if you're not with me. So I've decided I'm not going."

India's family wasn't wealthy—not even close. Dad was a

handyman who was often paid by neighbors in IOUs, second-hand clothes, and homemade jam. Money became even tighter when Mom quit her teaching job a few years back after Boo's asthma worsened to be with him at home, *just in case.*

"We'll find the money," Dad decided, pounding his fist on the table. "We did for the national bee, and we'll do it again."

India loved Dad's optimism, so she tried to let him down gently. "Raising enough money to go to Sydney was one thing, but how can we find enough to travel to London?"

"You leave that to me." Dad tapped his temple as if he had a grand plan.

"It's a lot of money, Arnie." Nanna Flo was a whiz at math. "With airfares, hotels, and taxis…I'd say we'd need at least…ten thousand dollars."

"That much, eh?" Dad's smile drooped, then he pushed aside his mug and looked into India's eyes. "This opportunity only happens to the very best. Maybe you're right. Maybe we can't afford for everyone to go, but that doesn't mean *you* have to miss out."

"It does," India argued. "I only had the courage to spell last time because you were all with me."

"Yes, but remember how you thought you weren't brave enough to even *enter*? Guess what. Turns out you were *more* than brave enough!"

"Your dad's right." Nanna Flo pointed at India. "You're as brave as a bull ant, and you need to be there."

"And I want the world to know how smart my sister is," Boo said.

"You do *want* to go, don't you?" Mom checked.

"Yes," India had to admit. She wanted to stand onstage with the world's best—to see if, maybe, she could even win.

"That's settled then!" Dad sat back in his chair. "Now all you have to do is choose one of us to be your chaperone, and we can start planning what to pack."

It sounded simple, but the idea of traveling to England without all her family made India feel as if she were standing on the edge of a very tall cliff.

"But who will I choose?"

"That's for you to decide," Mom said.

"Does that mean I can go?" Boo sparked up hopefully.

"Nice try, buddy." Dad tousled his hair. "But a chaperone has to be someone older, preferably with a driver's license."

Boo shrugged. "It was worth a try."

An uneasy silence followed, until Nanna Flo spoke up. "I've got it. As much as I'd love to go to England—with all those fancy castles and yummy pork pies—I think you should take your mother or father. They've worked their backsides off to get you this far, and I think they deserve to see you shine."

"But I'll miss you if you're not there."

"You'll be back before you know it." Nanna Flo was trying to be brave, but the Wimples knew she'd miss India too.

"I won't hear of it," Mom said. "It should be your father or Nanna Flo. I need to stay here to take care of Boo."

The thought of this made India's stomach tighten. "But I've never been that far away from you before. Or Boo."

Mom tried to answer, but then she frowned, and her mouth clamped shut.

"I have the answer," Dad said. "You should take your mom or Nanna Flo. It'll be a trip for the girls." He hugged Boo. "Us boys will stay here, look after the fort, and do manly stuff."

Boo wasn't sure what "manly stuff" meant, but considering how clumsy Dad was with tools, he was a little scared.

India slumped in her chair as if she were about to be swallowed whole. The Wimples were only trying to help, but she was even more confused than ever.

Mom kissed her on the forehead. "Whatever you decide will be fine by all of us."

This didn't lift India's mood. In fact, it made her feel a little worse, because she knew her mom meant it. India's family was the most important thing to her, her anchor in rough seas, and here was her mom saying it was OK to go to the other side of the world without them.

India felt sick. She used to feel this way a lot before the Stupendously Spectacular Spelling Bee. Even the smallest things would make her anxious—giving a speech in class, adults talking to her in the supermarket, the evening news on the television. Sometimes even answering the phone made her feel nauseous.

"There's always Skype," Mom said, still trying to sound cheerful. "We can see each other and talk every day."

"Or when you need to practice," Nanna Flo added.

"Or when you'd like to hear Mom tell more stories of *Brave Boo and Ingenious India*," Boo said.

"Or I could sing you to sleep," Dad said. There was an awkward pause. No one dared tell Dad his singing actually kept the neighborhood awake. "It'll be just like we're there."

This is called a white lie: a small, harmless untruth that is sometimes told to protect a person's feelings or make someone feel better. The Wimples knew it wouldn't be so simple, and Dad had only said it to cheer India up.

~~~~~

Long after the house had settled into sleep, India rolled over in bed. Boo's night-light in the hall cast a glow over everything.

One of the best days of her life had quickly became one of the most difficult. How was she supposed to choose? How could she pick Mom over Dad or leave Nanna Flo behind?

And what about Boo?

Every night since Mom and Dad had brought him home from the hospital when he was born, India had always been across the hall from him. She'd sometimes sneak into his room and watch his chest rise and fall or even wake on the floor beside his bed, not remembering how she'd gotten there.

She'd never in her whole life been far from him, and now she faced with going to the opposite side of the world.

There were so many words to describe how she felt.

Disheartened.

Despairing.

Desolate.

She looked at her bedside clock, which was something she did a lot when she felt anxious. Mom sometimes said if she watched the clock and counted the seconds as they passed, her eyes would slowly close, and she would fall into a deep sleep—that, or count sheep—but nothing was working.

That's when she heard Boo cough.

As always, India threw back her blankets and flew to Boo's room, ready to take out his inhaler and make sure he followed the right steps to avoid a full-blown asthma attack, but as she stood above him, Boo snuffled sleepily, rolled over, and settled back into a peaceful sleep.

And that's when it became clear: she couldn't leave Boo behind. How was she supposed to protect him when she was so far away?

That was it. She wasn't going to London.

Not without him.

As soon as she decided this, she felt lighter and heavier at the same time—lighter because she *couldn't* disappoint anyone from her family or travel to London without them, but a sadness also sank into her, weighing her down.

A single tear rolled down her cheek, and she tiptoed back to her room.

From her small bed in Yungabilla, she stared through the window at the night sky sprinkled with stars. She wondered what it would have been like to fly to England—to see Big Ben, the Tower of London, and maybe Buckingham Palace—or even the Queen herself. She knew about the city's famous landmarks because she'd studied them in school, and she had a feeling they would be even more spectacular in real life.

And there was something else.

Something she hadn't mentioned to anyone.

The most marvelous part of going to London would be seeing Rajish again.

They had met during the national spelling bee. India remembered his infectious grin that lifted into the corners of his cheeks, making everyone around him smile (and at first had made India want to run). She'd never been good at making friends, but with him, it felt easy. They'd been writing letters since they last saw each other. *Paper* letters, not email, which somehow felt more special. She'd kept each one in her bedside table.

She let herself think about him a moment longer before brushing the thought away.

She pulled the blankets to her chin and closed her eyes against another threatening tear, knowing that this was the most difficult decision she'd ever faced and that she wouldn't be going to London after all.

3
AVARICIOUS
(adjective):

Greedy, covetous, money-grabbing.

Their avaricious nature meant they loved money above everything else.

MEANWHILE, ON THE OTHER SIDE of the world, in a small suburb of Toronto, Canada, a young girl named Holly Trifle was having her own troubles.

She was lying on her narrow, lumpy bed with the door closed, reading a book. Her bedroom wasn't so much a room as it was a big closet where families put stuff they weren't sure they wanted but keep around just in case. It had no windows, so even on a sunny day, Holly had to have the light on, which highlighted just how tiny the room actually was.

But to Holly, it was the most glorious place in the world. Not even Wonderland Funpark or the city library were more glorious. She loved being there, because there was never any danger her family would come in. If she stayed quiet enough, they often seemed to forget she was even there.

Which was just the way she liked it.

It wasn't that Holly didn't like her family, but she often wondered if they were her *real* family or if she'd been given to them by mistake when she was born.

Her mother felt the same way, because when the nurse had tried to hand the newborn Holly to Mrs. Trifle, she'd shouted, *"No! She can't be my baby! There must be some mistake."*

Mrs. Trifle had howled about how a pregnancy that had felt so blissful could have produced such a hideously plain child. She'd followed all the advice on YouTube: She'd eaten her greens and meditated to the sound of groaning whales. She'd drunk water from the Himalayas and taken long walks in the woods.

But it hadn't worked!

When the nurse had placed Holly in the crib beside her mother's bed, she'd reached out, gurgling, ready to be cuddled.

But Mrs. Trifle was having none of it.

"Take her away!" she'd shouted. "And do *not* let anyone see her. I don't want them traumatized by such a terrifying sight."

Mr. Trifle had thought his daughter looked perfect with her button nose and chubby legs. He couldn't quite see what all the fuss was about.

"I think she looks just fine."

"Fine!" Mrs. Trifle had screeched. "Fine isn't good enough!

Benedict and Gertrude were born with long lashes and angelic curls." Mrs. Trifle had scowled at the bald-headed baby staring at her. "This one looks like a shriveled prune!"

Benedict and Gertrude were children from Mrs. Trifle's first marriage. Now adults, Benedict was a personal trainer, and Gertrude was a Pilates instructor and a soon-to-be-famous actress—if only someone would give her a role. To Mrs. Trifle, *they* were perfect.

Unlike Holly.

"All babies go through this squishy phase," Mr. Trifle had said. "When she's a little older, she'll be as beautiful as the others."

"What if she isn't?" Mrs. Trifle had lamented. "What if she looks like *that* forever?"

Two passersby had peeked into the room, wondering what all the screaming was about and if they should call a nurse.

Mrs. Trifle had known they'd stopped to stare at the frightful child. "We have to leave." She had begun to gather her things. "Before someone mistakes her for a hairless dog."

Mr. Trifle had carefully scooped Holly into his arms. In that instant, he was struck by her wide, curious eyes and rosy cheeks. She'd tapped his nose with her tiny fingers and gurgled some more. He'd taken her hand in his and smiled in wonder at his first child.

"Are you coming, or do I leave you both behind?"

Mr. Trifle had been snapped back to reality by Mrs. Trifle's temper. "Yes, dear," he'd sighed.

His wife hadn't always been like this. When they'd first met, he'd been dazzled by her easy laugh and exuberance, but over time, she'd laughed less and had a tendency to overreact. Even though he would never tell her that for fear she would...overreact.

They had snuck out of the hospital down the fire stairs. Mrs. Trifle had worn sunglasses and a scarf and kept her head low all the way to the car as she despaired about what she had done to deserve such a child.

"We've been good people," she'd wailed. "We've never thrown garbage into our neighbor's yard or been cruel to homeless people—we step over them like you're supposed to—and yet..." She had sniffed. "*This* happened."

"There, there," Mr. Trifle had tried to comfort his wife while also trying to avoid her arms, which were wheeling around in distress. He'd strapped Holly into her baby seat. She'd murmured and blown raspberries.

Mrs. Trifle had caught a glimpse of Holly in the rearview mirror. She'd shuddered and looked away. "And now we're stuck with this...reject."

Yes, she actually said that.

Mrs. Trifle called Holly a *reject*.

"Oh why? *Why?*" She'd sobbed.

Mr. Trifle knew that when his wife worked herself into this state, there was no way to calm her down, so he'd sped home as fast as he could.

No matter how much Mrs. Trifle hoped that her daughter would grow to become beautiful, it didn't work. Her face remained plain, and no matter the effort her mother went to to style Holly's lifeless, mousy-colored hair and dress her in expensive clothes, it came out all wrong. Holly was doomed to be ordinary.

As she grew older, Holly realized she had almost nothing in common with her family. She *must* belong to different parents—parents who were kind and clever, who read books, daydreamed, and memorized interesting facts, just like her. Parents who volunteered at soup kitchens for the homeless and never, ever ignored them or stepped over them.

Holly was thinking these thoughts as she lay in her room that was almost a room, only yards away from where Mr. and Mrs. Trifle and Gertrude and Benedict were watching the latest commercial for the family fitness business: Beaut Butts and Guts.

The music blared on the television, with all four Trifles

dressed in workout clothes, running, squatting, and stretching. Mr. Trifle stood in the center, lifting a dumbbell with one hand.

"We here at Beaut Butts and Guts believe everyone can be beautiful. In the expert hands of the Trifle family, you will soon be the very best YOU that you can be. So call 1-800-BUTTS, and say goodbye to that baggy butt forever."

The doorbell rang. The real Trifles ignored it while the Trifles in the commercial pointed at the screen and said in unison, *"Because Beaut Butts and Guts are waiting for you."*

The Trifles cheered at how magnificent they were until Gertrude shouted, "Let's watch it again!"

The doorbell rang a second time.

Holly poked her head out of her room. "Would you like me to get the door?"

Like most times when Holly spoke, none of her family paid any attention to her.

"I guess that means yes." Holly pushed her reading glasses up and climbed out of her room. She opened the door to the mailman. He held a letter in a cream-colored envelope with swirling gold lettering, and it was sealed with a red wax crest.

"Oh my goodness!" Holly's long braids jiggled as she looked at the letter.

"This is for you," he said. "It seems important. I can feel it." The mailman smiled at her in a way that rarely happened in her family—the kind of smile that gives you a warm, toasty feeling inside.

"Thank you," she said, for the letter but more so for the smile.

Holly wiggled a finger under the seal and opened it. Her palms began to sweat, and her hands began to shake. She read the words over and over, hardly able to believe it was true.

She hurried into the living room, clutching the letter in front of her, and waited for the Trifles to finish watching their commercial. Again.

"I have exciting news," Holly said.

The Trifles looked up, annoyed that she was interrupting their plans for another viewing, until they saw the ornate letter.

Mrs. Trifle brightened. "Is it the prime minister asking me to be the national ambassador for fitness? Heaven knows we need one, with all those flabby bottoms out there."

"No," Holly said. "It's not that."

"Is it the television station?" Mr. Trifle asked. "Replying to my emails about a Beaut Butts and Guts reality show?"

Holly shook her head. "No, I'm afraid it's not—"

"I know!" Gertrude Trifle sprang forward. "It's a Hollywood studio begging me to appear in their action film."

"I'm sorry," Holly said. "But it's—"

"The World's Hunkiest Bachelor competition." Benedict smiled smugly. "I knew they'd want me."

"No, it's not that, either."

Mrs. Trifle was confused. "Well, what else could it be?"

Holly took a steadying breath. "I've been invited to compete in the Most Marvelous International Spelling Bee in London."

The Trifles said nothing, unable to see how *this* was exciting news.

"What?" Mrs. Trifle asked. "You mean that spelling competition you lost last time?"

"I didn't lose." Holly felt her excitement fade, which is

something that happened a lot when she was with her family. "I came second."

"Exactly!" Her mother said in a huff. "Which means you *lost.*"

"Second place is the first-place loser," Benedict chimed in.

"It was a very *close* second," Mr. Trifle said, trying to defend his daughter.

Benedict sniffed. "All those years spent in your room reading books, and you couldn't even win."

"Books!" Gertrude said. "They're a waste of money, if you ask me." Not that anyone *had* asked her, and since Gertrude had never read a book in her life, she really wasn't an expert on the subject.

Even though Holly had lived with her family for eleven years, four months, and three days, this wasn't quite the reaction she was hoping for, but what Mrs. Trifle said next was something she was absolutely not expecting.

"You're not going."

"What?" Holly momentarily lost her breath. "I *have* to go. The top spellers from around the world have been invited."

"Well, they'll be there without you." Mrs. Trifle stood up and put her manicured hands on her shiny, Spandex-clad hips. "You're not going to some *spelling contest* halfway across the world when it's time you helped in the family business. Your brother and sister do their share, so I don't see why you shouldn't too."

Holly started to panic. "But—"

"That's right! *Butts!* Every waking second you're not at school, you're going to be focused on butts—not on some silly competition where last time, you were too *lazy* to win and blew our chances at a great big bag of prize money."

"Prize money." Benedict's ears pricked up at the mention of money. "Since this is the international spelling bee, there'll be even *more.*"

"More?" Mrs. Trifle's avaricious eyes widened. "How much more?" She snatched the invitation from her daughter's hands. "Dear Ms. Trifle, we hereby invite you…blah, blah, blah… congratulations, spelling, blah… Here it is!" She paused for a second. "Ten thousand dollars."

"I think she should enter," Benedict said.

Holly smiled. This was the nicest thing her brother had ever done for her, even though it was only because of the motorcycle and leather jacket he was thinking about buying with all that cash.

"It could be another waste of time if she bombs again," Mrs. Trifle sneered.

Holly's mother's words felt like an anchor dragging her down into some murky gloom.

Mr. Trifle caught a glimpse of his daughter's miserable face and knew it was time to step in. "Or all that free publicity could make Beaut Butts and Guts the number one fitness center in the country. And it would fulfill our dream of expanding the business overseas. What do you say? Should we let her try again?"

Mrs. Trifle considered the idea. "It would give her a chance to redeem herself from the previous failure."

Coming second in a national spelling bee wasn't *actually* a failure, but Holly could feel her mother changing her mind, so she didn't bother to argue.

"All right. Molly can enter."

Mrs. Trifle didn't realize that she'd just called her daughter the wrong name. This was not, as you've probably guessed, the first time this had happened. She glared at her youngest child, leaned down, and poked a glossy fingernail against Holly's chest. "This time, we'll be there to make sure you don't blow it."

Holly froze. "Actually, the competition will only pay for one chaperone, so I was thinking Dad could come with me."

"It'll be better if we're both there," Mrs. Trifle decided. "We'll need both of us if we're going to expand to Britain."

Holly had to think fast. "What about the business here?"

"Gertrude and Benedict can be in charge." Mrs. Trifle gazed proudly at her favored children. "They're more than capable."

And with that, the Trifles went back to watching their commercial. Again.

Holly shuddered at the idea of her mother coming to the bee. Mrs. Trifle seemed to make it her life's aim to embarrass her daughter, performing aerobic routines at sports events and doing leg lunges while pushing the shopping cart. She even made the family ride the bus so she could hand Beaut Butts and Guts flyers to the overweight passengers.

Mrs. Trifle was so embarrassing that Holly's friends had long ago stopped coming over after school in case they got one of her mother's lectures.

Now she'd have the opportunity to embarrass Holly in another country, on the world stage.

Holly's initial excitement had almost disappeared, and she wondered if she should even go.

But that made her feel worse.

Staying in her room and reading would save Holly from any embarrassment, but she also knew that being part of the Most Marvelous International Spelling Bee would be a way to meet people who were more like her.

Or even make a friend who might want to hear what she had to say.

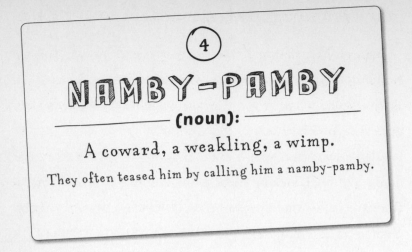

4
NAMBY-PAMBY

(noun):

A coward, a weakling, a wimp.

They often teased him by calling him a namby-pamby.

IN A DRAB APARTMENT ON a dead-end street in Wormwood, England, a child named Peter Eriksson lived with his mom and grandfather.

He sat on his bed, staring at the gray street below. Gray apartment buildings were squished tightly on both sides, and the whole neighborhood was soaked by a steady drizzle of rain.

The boy's pet lizard, Prince Harry, snuggled on his chest.

"At least he didn't punch me in the face this time." The brand-new bruise on Peter's stomach ached. "I guess that's something."

Prince Harry stretched out his neck and nuzzled Peter's cheek, making him laugh. "If only you were bigger, you'd stand up to him. I know it."

That day, after school, Peter had been bullied.

Again.

Bruiser had slammed him against the brick wall of the building. There'd been an icy chill to the day, which made the bricks feel even harder and sharper, and Peter knew they'd leave another bruise he'd have to hide from his mom.

The playground was empty, and a cold wind had blown across the yard, kicking up litter. There was something about the way they swirled against the cloud-filled sky that made Peter wish he were a scrap of paper too, so he could float away, light and free.

"Well? What've you got to say?"

Peter had been dragged away from his daydream by the tightening grip of Bruiser's fingers, which had held him by the scruff of his shirt.

"You gonna answer me, Chubby, or not?"

Chubby. That's what Peter was called at school—even by some of the teachers. They said it with a smile, as if it were a joke, but he never understood why they didn't realize how much it hurt. At least the bruises faded over time.

"Why didn't your dad come to the father-son breakfast?"

Every year, the school had a special breakfast for fathers and sons. Every year, Peter's father never showed up.

Bruiser knew why, but he enjoyed watching Peter squirm as he tried to think of an answer.

The truth was this: it had been eight years since Peter's father had left.

Two thousand nine hundred and twenty-two days since he had decided Peter and his mom weren't worth staying around for.

Seventy thousand one hundred and twenty-eight hours since he had walked out the front door, leaving his muddy footprints on the carpet and a giant, father-shaped hole.

Most nights, as Peter lay in bed beneath the glow of the streetlight through his curtains, he thought of his dad. He wondered what he was doing and if he had other kids. He wondered if his dad ever thought about him and his mom, even for just a moment, or maybe on Peter's birthday.

Every year on his birthday, while his mom was making a special breakfast of pancakes, blackberries, and extra whipped cream, Peter would listen for the clink of the mailbox. When he heard it, his heart raced, and his thoughts ran together in a jumble.

Maybe this was the year his dad would remember.

Maybe this year, he'd send a present.

Maybe he'd apologize for all the other years he hadn't been able to send presents, because he'd been on great adventures all over the world, in remote locations with no mail carriers to deliver the dozens of letters he'd written, telling Peter how special he was and how he'd soon come back and say he was wrong for leaving, and they'd be a family again.

Every year, Peter would stand at the mailbox, take a deep breath, and open the squeaky lid…only to find it full of bills and flyers for gyms or Chinese restaurants.

Every year.

This was what he had thought about as Bruiser's thick bucket head and wire-brush hair leaned over him.

"Is it because your dad left after he found out you were a *loser*?"

Peter had stared at Bruiser's crooked sneer and done what he always did in these situations. He'd lied.

"He's a brilliant surgeon, busy saving lives."

Sometimes Peter's dad was a firefighter, like his grandpop, other times a paramedic, but he was always a hero.

Peter had known exactly what was coming next.

What always happened.

He'd tensed his stomach, making it as hard as he could before Bruiser landed a punch that had doubled him over and crumbled him to his knees, leaving him gasping for breath.

"*Namby-pamby.*" Bruiser had chuckled and shuffled away.

Peter had rolled onto his side, the hurtful words ringing in his ears.

Bruiser had called him a namby-pamby from the first day of school. The parents had been invited to the classroom as a special welcoming treat, but when it was time for them to leave, Peter had clung to his mom and cried.

He couldn't help it. What if she never came back? What if she disappeared like his dad?

Bruiser had waited for her to go before he hissed through a cruel smile, "*Namby-pamby.*"

It was an insult Bruiser used when he needed to add an extra sting to his punch. And it always worked.

When Peter was able to stand without his stomach hurting too much, he'd begun the slow walk home.

As he'd approached his house, he had seen his grandfather waiting inside the gate. He'd been out of breath and waving something in the air.

Peter had walked faster, worried that something was wrong—that Grandpop was sick, or his mom had been hurt, or...

"Peter, my boy, this arrived for you this morning." He'd handed over a cream-colored envelope with swirling gold lettering, sealed with a red wax crest.

"I'm not sure what it is." Grandpop Eriksson's silver, wispy hair coiled around his head like cotton candy. His shirt had been crumpled and his sweater had been buttoned all wrong, like he'd been thinking about something else while getting dressed, which often happened with Grandpop Eriksson. "It seems very important. I can feel it."

Peter had taken the envelope. "What do you think it is?"

"We won't know until you open it, but you'll have to be quick—my old heart can't wait much longer."

Peter had carefully opened the letter. He'd stared at the words on the page.

"It's...it's..."

"Yes? *Yes?*"

"An invitation to..."

"*Yes?*"

Peter had found it hard to find the words, even though they were right there in front of him.

"The Most Marvelous International Spelling Bee in London."

"Woo-hoo!" Peter's grandfather had thrown his fists into the air and swept his arms around his grandson, the letter squished between them. "I *knew* it was something great. I'll call your mom. She'll want to buy something on the way home to celebrate." He'd hurried to the house and cried out, "My grandson's going to London!"

Peter had stared at the letter. It wasn't the one he'd been hoping for all these years, the one that might never arrive, but this one was pretty good. As he'd stood on the path, a twinge of pain gripping his stomach, he'd smiled for the first time that day.

He was going to London.

Peter Eriksson of Dreary Lane, Wormwood, was going to London, far from Bruiser and the taunts of the kids and teachers.

Far from being a namby-pamby.

But there was something else even more important than that.

As Peter sat on his bed in his boring bedroom, stroking Prince Harry, he said, "The Most Marvelous International Spelling Bee is broadcast on TV, so maybe Dad will be watching."

Peter could see it now. His dad would be at home, having dinner in front of the TV, and he'd recognize something in one of the kids onstage—a dimple, or the way he walked, or the stubborn curl above his forehead that he could never comb down—and maybe, just maybe, he'd know it was his son.

"He'll see that I've grown up to be someone worthwhile, maybe even a champion. Then he'll have to come back. Don't you think, Prince Harry?"

The crested gecko placed a foot on Peter's cheek.

Peter snuggled him even closer and allowed himself another smile.

Maybe this time, his secret birthday wish would come true.

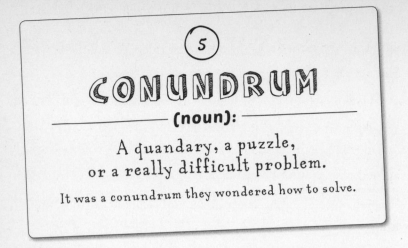

5

CONUNDRUM

—— (noun): ——

A quandary, a puzzle,
or a really difficult problem.

It was a conundrum they wondered how to solve.

THE WIMPLES SAT HUNCHED OVER their breakfasts. The clanging of spoons into bowls and the crunch of toast were all that could be heard over their melancholy mood.

Mom slurped her tea. Normally in situations where her family was feeling blue, she'd say something to cheer them up, which moms often do in families, but this morning, she couldn't, no matter how much she tried—not when her daughter was going to miss competing against the best spellers in the world.

India deserved to be there, but how could they afford to make it happen?

Nanna Flo buttered her toast, thinking the same thing, but she also wondered something else. If she hadn't broken her wrist enthusiastically attempting a yoga move and come to live with the Wimples, they'd have enough money for India to enter. She was sure of it.

She snuck a look at her granddaughter, knowing this was all her fault. What kind of grandmother did that?

Boo pushed his porridge around his bowl. He wouldn't have agreed with Nanna Flo one bit, because this was all *his* fault. If he didn't have asthma, Mom would still be teaching instead of homeschooling him. They'd have more than enough money for all of them to go to London.

But as terrible as they all felt, it was even worse for Dad.

He knew this was definitely *his* fault.

If only he was the hard-hitting journalist he had once been and not a handyman working for IOUs and secondhand clothes, they would all be going to London. What kind of dad was he when instead of breaking tough stories, he was unclogging toilets? And all while watching his daughter miss one of the most marvelous moments of her life.

Dad's worst fear was letting his kids down, and here he was, doing just that.

India glanced at her family, knowing their misery was all her fault, and she was determined to cheer them up.

"You know what? I'm OK about not going to London." This was one of those white lies, of course, but she desperately wanted to wipe the gloominess off their faces. "Really, I'm not disappointed at all."

It didn't work. Mostly because the Wimples knew she said it only to make them feel better, which made them all feel a little worse.

What a conundrum.

"Anyone home?" Daryl let himself in the back door. "Just came to say hello to Yungabilla's newest hero."

Daryl was in a fine mood, which is why it took him a little longer to realize that something was terribly wrong. He stared at the disappointed looks that swamped their faces.

"OK, what's wrong?"

No one knew how to break the news to Daryl.

India decided it was up to her. "I'm not going to London."

"What?!" Daryl's hands flew into the air. "Why not?"

"The competition will pay for me and one chaperone, and I won't go if we can't all go together."

"But you can't—"

"I'm sorry, Daryl." India did her best to sound firm. "I've made my decision, and there's no point trying to change my mind."

"But I think—"

"I know you mean well," India interrupted, "but the truth is I only just made it through the Stupendously Spectacular

Spelling Bee because my family was with me. How can I possibly choose one person to fly to London with me, knowing I was getting farther and farther away from the others every second? I'm not going, and I won't be talked out of it."

India crossed her arms and tried to look as defiant as she could, which wasn't very defiant, because she wasn't very good at that kind of thing.

A sly smile rose to Daryl's lips. "And that, India Wimple, is one reason this family is my favorite of all time. Of course you have to go together! It would be a *travesty* if you didn't!" He pulled out a chair and sat with them. "Now all we have to do is come up with an ingenious plan for making it happen."

"But how?" Dad scratched his head. "We need plane tickets, hotel rooms, cab fare... We don't have that kind of money, Daryl."

"Then we'll find it."

"Where?" India asked.

"That's what we're about to figure out." He pulled a small notebook from his pocket.

Daryl's enthusiasm made them all feel a little brighter.

"You're a good egg." Nanna Flo kissed him on the cheek, and Daryl blushed bright red. "Have been ever since you were a boy."

Over lots of cups of tea and steady servings of toast and jelly, Daryl and the Wimples came up with an ingenious plan.

~~~~~~~

Within twenty-four hours, the townsfolk of Yungabilla were gathered in the town hall. The Country Women's Association had set up a stall in the back, serving tea and scones with helpings of jam and cream—but no lamingtons—while a rowdy rabble of adults, kids, and animals waited their turn to be photographed.

The plan was this: the entire town would pose for the Yungabilla souvenir calendar, which would be sold online in a crowdfunding campaign that was sure to make a fortune.

Or, at the very least, send the Wimples to London.

Everyone pitched in, helping out with hair and makeup, arranging the lights and props so that each photograph looked unique and captured the spirit of the town. Dad set up his camera on a tripod, and Mom wrote down the order in which the groups would be photographed, while Nanna Flo used a loudspeaker to make sure everything ran smoothly.

"Thank you, everyone, for supporting India on her way to London," Nanna's voice boomed. "This is going to be a roaring success, or I'll eat my boots for breakfast."

First up was Farmer Austin, standing proudly beside Bessie, who was wearing her best winter coat and beanie with a freshly picked daisy bobbing from her ear.

Next came Mayor Bob, Mrs. Wild, and the kids from Yungabilla Primary School. They were dressed as Willy Wonka and the Oompa Loompas from last year's school play.

Gracie Hubbard posed as she was about to eat a spoonful of delicious cheesecake beside Mrs. O'Donnell, who sipped a frothy milkshake. The Country Firefighters wore bright yellow uniforms with a fire hose draped around them like a giant python. The Craft Society wore sweaters and hats they'd knitted themselves, and the local yoga club, led by Nanna Flo, demonstrated their best poses.

For the final photograph, everyone involved stood behind India and held up letters that spelled:

INDIA WIMPLE
SPELLING CHAMPION

Apart from Bessie eating up the last of the scones, it was a great success.

By the time the last of the locals had left the hall, it was well past midnight. Mom and Nanna Flo had driven a sleepy Boo to bed, while Dad and India locked the hall and began to walk home.

"Do you think it'll work?" India asked.

"Of course it will," Dad said. "Who wouldn't want to buy a

Yungabilla souvenir calendar? They'll sell so fast, all you'll have to worry about is what to pack."

India felt a shiver of excitement. Maybe she *would* be going to London after all—and she'd see Rajish.

Her stomach flipped. Not in that nervous, nauseous way that used to happen to India, but like a butterfly had been let loose in her stomach and was flapping its wings wildly.

As if Dad had been reading her mind, he said, "And you'll see Rajish again."

"Who?" India turned to Dad so quickly that she almost tripped.

"Rajish." Dad caught her by the arm. "You know, from the last spelling bee. We went to India on vacation together."

India hoped the darkness meant Dad couldn't see her cheeks, which she knew would be fiery red.

"Oh, *that* Rajish."

"How many boys called Rajish do you know?"

"I… We…" India was desperate to change the subject. "You did a great job with the photographs today."

"Thanks." Dad wrapped his arm around India's shoulder. "It was fun to get behind the camera again. It reminded me how much I enjoyed it."

Dad used to work at the local newspaper before it shut down.

"Do you miss being a journalist?"

He nodded. "I worked on some really interesting stories."

"Like when Yungabilla hosted the National Vanilla Custard Competition, or when the Tivoli sisters turned one hundred and celebrated by skinny-dipping in the lake."

Dad laughed. "They caused quite a stir." He stared off into the distance. "Some things aren't meant to last, I guess."

India knew Dad didn't quite believe that. "But you were so good at it."

Now it was Dad's turn to change the subject. "Race you home?"

And before India could answer, he was off.

"Hey! Not fair! You got a head start."

And with that, they ran through the quiet, lamp-lit streets of Yungabilla all the way home.

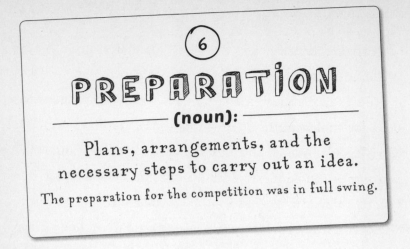

6

PREPARATION

(noun):

Plans, arrangements, and the necessary steps to carry out an idea.

The preparation for the competition was in full swing.

WHEN THE PRINTED CALENDARS ARRIVED, they were glossy and colorful, and everyone was convinced they were going to be a huge hit.

Boo put the final touches on the crowdfunding campaign before launching it into the world. All they had to do now was sit back and wait for the orders and donations to roll in. Daryl and the Wimples raised glasses of orange juice to toast its success.

But after ten days, the total amount raised had inched up to just four hundred dollars, which wasn't nearly enough to get them to London. Boo knew they needed another angle to make it go national.

Early one Saturday morning, while Nanna was at yoga, Dad was rebuilding their neighbor Elsie's chicken coop after her goat had rammed it to pieces, and Mom was delivering Meals on Wheels, Boo knew he had his chance.

He was never allowed out of the house unless he was with someone, not because there was anything to worry about in Yungabilla—it was as safe a town as you could ever visit—but mostly it was so he wasn't alone if he had an asthma attack.

Boo going anywhere alone would usually make Mom quite nervous. There'd be lots of questions about where he was going and when he'd be back until she decided it would be better if she went with him. Boo knew this was Mom's way of taking care of him, but this morning, there wasn't time for any of that.

After a quick phone call, he poked his head into India's room. "We have to go."

She looked up from her dictionary. "Where?"

"You'll see. Come on, or we'll be late." Boo knew he couldn't tell India what he was planning or she'd never agree to it.

Within minutes, they were walking down Main Street toward the Yungabilla Community Center. The hub housed the local government offices, post office, and the Yungabilla Tourist Information Bureau, all run by Mrs. Rahim.

Boo pushed open the glass doors. Mrs. Rahim at the counter greeted them with a smile.

"You can go right in. He's waiting for you."

"He who?" India asked.

"You'll find out." Boo strode down the corridor to the end of the building and stopped in front of a door with a sign that read:

RADIO YUNGABILLA
THE SWEET SOUNDS OF THE COUNTRY

India froze. "It's Macca."

Macca was a radio host her parents had listened to since she was a kid. His show was heard all over the country. Macca was famous.

"Yep, and he wants to talk to you."

"*Me?*" India was about to launch into all the reasons this was a bad idea when Boo put his fingers to his lips and opened the door to the radio booth.

Macca wore headphones and sat in front of a computer and a desk filled with buttons. He leaned into his microphone and waved Boo and India in to take a seat.

"And that was Dora Williams singing an old favorite, 'I Love You More Than I Love My Ute.'"

Boo and India sat at the microphone opposite him.

"Now, we're in for a special treat," Macca said. "Each year, the Stupendously Spectacular Spelling Bee finds Australia's best

speller, and the current champion is Yungabilla's very own India Wimple. I'm lucky to have India and her brother, Boo, here in the studio. Welcome to Radio Yungabilla."

India said nothing, so Boo spoke for both of them. "Thanks for having us, Macca."

"India, after winning the bee, how does it feel to be invited to London to compete with the world's best?"

Boo nudged India gently. "Good."

"How's the preparation going? You studying that dictionary?"

"Yes," she said.

Macca waited for her to say more. "I hear there might be a little bit of a hitch to competing."

It was at this point that Boo took over. "It's a great honor to be part of the international bee, but we need to raise money to get there. We've started a crowdfunding page where people can donate whatever they can, but anyone who gives more than fifteen dollars will receive a Yungabilla souvenir calendar."

"Now there's a deal you can't resist, listeners. My fifteen dollars bought me my own copy, and it really is something. I donated a photo of me sitting on my 1954 vintage John Deere tractor. Do you think you'll reach your goal?"

"We have to!" Boo said. "India deserves to be there. She's one of the smartest people I know. And the kindest. I have asthma, which can get pretty scary, but India has always been there for me, and now it's my turn to be there for her."

"You think your sister's pretty special."

Boo paused. He thought of all the times India had woken up next to him or rushed to his side whenever he coughed and how she nearly gave up her spot in the Stupendously Spectacular Spelling Bee Grand Final when he wasn't well. "She's the best sister a brother could have. Sorry to all the other sisters out there."

Macca laughed. "Well, that's good enough for me. So what do you say, listeners? Your fifteen dollars will get you a calendar and can help send Australia's spelling champion to London.

India, we wish you all the best and know you'll make our country proud."

Boo spent the rest of the day hovering over Mom's phone, waiting for the donations to roll in.

The hours ticked by. Little by little, the total increased. When night fell, Dad poked his head into Boo's room. "How's it going?"

"Getting there. Slowly."

Dad saw a flicker of disappointment on Boo's face before Boo turned back to the screen.

Much later, when India crept into Boo's room (as she often did), she found him asleep, still clutching the phone. She carefully slid it from his fingers and placed it on his bedside table.

When she tiptoed back to her room, she saw a small glow through her curtains. It was coming from the shed. Inside was Dad. The light from his computer made his face look ghostly pale. He slumped forward and cradled his head in his hands.

India slipped into her sneakers and crept outside across the yard. She peeked in the door and saw the table covered in papers.

"You're up late."

Dad flinched, surprised to hear a voice in the darkness. "You too."

"I couldn't sleep."

Dad held out his arm, and India slipped into his hug. "You OK?"

India nodded. "What are they?"

Dad shuffled the papers into a messy pile. "Nothing important."

India could tell that wasn't true and that they were in fact *very* important.

"Nice try, Dad, but I've known you for over eleven years. You're not good at fibbing."

"OK." Dad sighed. "I've been writing articles and stories ever since the paper shut down. I send them to news agencies all over the country, and they send me these rejections."

India pulled one from the top.

Dear Mr. Wimple,

Thank you for submitting your article. Unfortunately, the subject of your story isn't interesting enough for our readers.

India frowned and read another.

Dear Mr. Wimple,

While we like your style, your piece isn't quite right for our website.

India wanted to shout at them all. "They're wrong."

"Wrong or not," Dad said, "they don't want me to write for them." He took the rejection letters and put them in a box beside him. "Can I tell you a secret?"

India nodded.

"Working at the paper was the only thing I ever felt really good at." He sighed. "But maybe even that's not true."

"It *is* true!" India cried. "Plus, you're good at lots of things."

Dad held up his bandaged thumb. "Really? Tell that to Elsie's goat."

"OK, sometimes there's an accident, but what about being the best dad in the world?"

Dad laughed. "I'm not sure even that's true."

"It is for me! You've read stories to Boo and me every night since we were babies, and you tell the best dad jokes when we're sad."

Dad looked down. "But I can't get you to London."

India snuggled closer. "I don't need to go. I like being here with you in Yungabilla. Can you read me some of your stories?"

Dad shook his head. "They're no good, India."

"Please?"

Dad couldn't refuse India's pleading look. "All right," he said, taking a story from the pile, "but don't complain when you realize the rejection letters are right."

India listened intently as Dad read. He was nervous at first and kept tripping over his words, but as he continued to read, he became more confident.

And the story was good! Really good. It had everything India wanted in a story: vivid details, clever twists, interesting characters with big hearts, and it kept her fascinated till the very end.

"Can you read another?"

"You're not just being nice?"

"As a dedicated bookworm, I know a good story when I hear one, and I'd like another, please."

Dad read to India by the light of the computer—stories about people overcoming tragedy, small heroic acts, and scientific discoveries that could change the world. India never wanted them to end.

Just as Dad was about to read another, they heard a cry from the house. They knew instantly who it was.

"Boo," India said.

Dad threw his story aside, and they raced from the shed and across the yard. He yanked open the screen door and hurried into Boo's room. "Are you OK?"

Boo was sitting up in bed. He was panting, and his eyes were wide. "I…"

Mom flew through the door and took the inhaler from his bedside table. "Is it another attack?"

"I…"

Nanna Flo rushed to Boo's side and rubbed his back, trying to keep her voice calm. "Don't worry, sweetie. We'll have you better in no time."

"It's not an attack!" Boo cried.

The Wimples stopped their fussing.

"It isn't?" India asked.

"Nope." The phone was in Boo's lap. "We've had a few more donations."

"How many more?" Dad asked.

"Quite a few." Boo wore a knowing smile.

Nanna Flo was almost too scared to ask. "How much do we have?"

Boo paused to build up the suspense. "Eleven thousand three hundred and forty-six dollars."

The Wimples stared at Boo as his words sank in.

"But that's more than our goal," Mom realized.

"How?" India worried she was in one of those dreams where something happens that you *really* want to happen, but in the end, you're disappointed because it's only a dream.

"Macca put the interview on his Facebook page, and it's been shared over one thousand times. People from all over Australia have donated. Even from overseas."

"That means…" Mom giggled. She couldn't help herself.

"Yep!" Boo gleamed with delight. "We are going to London."

Dad ruffled Boo's hair. "You are officially a genius."

"It was a team effort." Boo nodded.

"That's the Wimple spirit for you," Nanna Flo said. "There's no stopping us."

Dad jumped up from the bed and whisked India into the air. "We're going to London!" He swirled her around while the others ducked. "The Wimple family is going to London!"

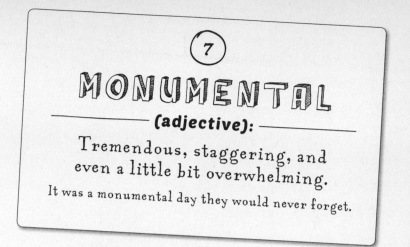

7

MONUMENTAL

(adjective):

Tremendous, staggering, and even a little bit overwhelming.

It was a monumental day they would never forget.

ALL AROUND THE WORLD, CONTESTANTS from the Most Marvelous International Spelling Bee were staying up late and waking up early, practicing every chance they could. They read dictionaries, held mock spelling bees, and watched past competitions online. They even dreamed about spelling.

Time flew, as it often does, and soon, the day of departure arrived.

In Toronto, Canada, Holly straightened her dress and gave herself one last look in the mirror. "You can do this, Holly Trifle."

Holly often did this. Because her family never seemed interested, she was her own cheerleading squad, along with Grandma Trifle, who often sent her emails and cards. And even though it felt lonely having a cheerleading squad of two, it helped when she felt nervous.

Maybe today, though, her parents *would* be excited. Maybe they'd have words of support—words of wisdom and love. After all, it wasn't every day your daughter was invited to compete in an international competition televised to millions around the world.

Today was a monumental day.

Today would be different.

Today, her parents would finally be on her side.

"Molly!" Mrs. Trifle screeched from the driveway below. "We're leaving without you if you don't get down here right now."

Or maybe not.

Holly tried to give herself another cheerleading squad smile, but this time, it didn't work. She picked up her purse and walked downstairs to the car.

Gertrude stared openmouthed at her half sister. "What are you wearing?"

Benedict laughed. "Is that one of Mom's tablecloths?"

"It's a dress." Holly held her arms out. "Grandma Trifle sent it to me."

"Who?" Gertrude asked.

"Grandma Trifle."

"I thought she was dead."

"She's not dead. She lives in Vancouver," Holly said.

Gertrude gave a petulant sneer, annoyed that no one had bothered to tell her. "News to me."

"She must be old." Benedict perked up. "Maybe I should be nice to her so she'll leave me money in her will."

"I wouldn't bother," Mrs. Trifle said and waved her hand. "She's as poor as a church mouse. Her house actually smells of mice, if I remember correctly, but it's been a few years since I've been there."

"It smells fine," Holly argued.

Holly often spent school vacations with Grandma Trifle while the rest of the Trifles were busy running the business, so she knew what her house smelled like. It was true that Grandma didn't have much, but her house was cozy and warm and always smelled of baked chicken or apple pie. Never mice.

"Anyway, you can't go out in that dress." Mrs. Trifle applied hot-pink lipstick to her pouting lips. "It looks like the cat coughed up a fur ball and dragged it through some paint."

Mr. Trifle was loading multiple suitcases and boxes into the trunk of the car. "I think the dress looks nice."

"It's awful," Mrs. Trifle corrected him.

"I like it," Holly said.

"What does *that* have to do with anything?" Mrs. Trifle really had no idea.

"I just thought—"

"Save your thoughts for spelling. People judge you by how you look, and if you wear that, they'll think you're a homeless child with parents who don't care."

Holly looked down at her dress. She liked the bright red flowers and the careful way Grandma had sewn orange buttons on each pocket. It was one of her favorite dresses, partly because the colors made her feel happy, but mostly because it was given to her on her tenth birthday, which only Grandma remembered.

Mrs. Trifle stared at her reflection in the side mirror of the car and dabbed at the corners of her shiny lips. "This family prides itself on how we present ourselves to the world, and I won't have you embarrassing us with that homemade sack. Now run up to your room and change, or we'll miss our flight."

Holly knew there was no point in arguing. "Yes, Mom," she said, doing exactly as she was told, just as she always did.

In her room, she folded Grandma's dress into a neat square and tucked it carefully into her bottom drawer. "I'll make you proud, Grandma. I promise."

~~~~~

In Wormwood, England, Peter's mother stood on the sidewalk with her son and father, waiting anxiously for a taxi. "And do you have your train ticket?"

"Yes, Mom." Peter was nervous too, but he tried to sound calm so his mother wouldn't worry even more.

"And your toothbrush?"

"Got it."

"I should get you more underwear. You can never have enough underwear."

She was about to turn to go back inside when Peter said, "We'll be fine, Mom. If we need anything, we'll get it in London."

Peter's mother held her son's cheeks. "I'm so proud of you, Peter. Have I told you that?"

"About ten times this morning."

"I'm sorry I can't come with you. It's a busy time at the warehouse."

"We'll be fine."

Peter turned to Grandpop, who was looking at the house as if all he wanted to do was run back inside and shut the door against the world. Grandpop hadn't been out much since Grandma died three years ago. He was a tall man with a spark in his eye, but losing Grandma had made his shoulders hunch and took away that spark. He'd become quiet and withdrawn.

Peter knew Grandpop was uneasy about going to London, but when he'd asked him to be his chaperone, he had agreed instantly, which made Peter love him even more.

They all stood there feeling a little afraid. Peter's mother was worried about them being so far away, Grandpop was worried he'd have one of his health problems and not be able to breathe, and Peter worried if they didn't leave soon, his mother might not let him go.

He was going to need to be strong for all of them.

"We'll be OK, won't we, Grandpop?"

Peter's question seemed to wake the old man up. He looked at his grandson's eager face. "Yeah," he said a little shakily before adding, "of course we will."

Luckily, at that moment, the taxi turned into the street and stopped beside them.

Peter's mother hugged her son. "Are you *sure* you have enough underwear?"

"I have everything I need," Peter said, even though it wasn't quite true. He loved his mom and his granddad and their life in the drab apartment, but there were two things he wanted more than anything: for the bullying to stop and for his dad to come back.

But he would never say this out loud. Instead, he stood as tall as he could and said, "I'll make you proud, Mom."

Unfortunately, what was supposed to make his mom feel better made her cry even more.

She hugged him tighter. "You always do."

Peter sent Grandpop a *rescue me* look.

"We better go, Maggie," Grandpop said, "or we'll miss our train."

Peter waved to his mom as they drove away, past the gray apartments, the broken fences, and the litter lying on the sidewalk.

He would never, ever tell his mom, but leaving made him feel light and happy. For ten whole days, he wouldn't be picked on or punched or called a namby-pamby. For ten whole days, he'd be far away from it all.

It was going to be monumental.

~~~~~

In Yungabilla, Australia, Boo and India crouched outside their parents' bedroom door. Mom had been nervous for weeks about their trip, and the day of their departure was no better.

"London is a big city," she told Dad, "which means more pollution and asthma attacks, so we have to be prepared."

When it came to Boo's asthma, Mom was always prepared, but being on a plane for so long, far away from medical attention, made her anxious.

Dad was doing his best to calm her down. "He'll be fine. I'm sure of it."

"How can you be sure after what happened last time?" Mom snapped.

India flinched. Mom *never* snapped at Dad.

By "last time," she meant Boo's asthma attack before the Stupendously Spectacular Spelling Bee Grand Final—the one that sent him to hospital and they thought he might not survive.

Dad remembered it well. He sometimes had nightmares about it.

"Just being somewhere new can trigger an asthma attack, or dust mites in pillows, or changes in temperature. What if it happens again?" Mom asked.

The Wimples had lived with these questions since Boo was young: *What if the next asthma attack was even worse? What if they weren't prepared? What if he didn't make it?*

Dad's voice was calm and sure. "I've called the hotel in London and let them know about Boo. They've sent me details of the nearest hospital, doctor, and pharmacy. We have his medical records if anyone needs them, and we have his bag of medication. The moment Boo doesn't feel well, we'll be on it."

Boo slowly got up and tiptoed back to his room.

India followed and sat on his bed beside him. "I've never heard her so worried."

"She doesn't need to be," Boo said. "I have my asthma plan

and inhaler, and Dr. Fiona said I'm fine for me to travel." He sighed. "I'm not a baby anymore, India."

"I'm sorry if we're a little over the top sometimes."

"Can I tell you something?"

"Anything," India said.

"I want to go back to school."

"Have you told Mom?"

"No, but she misses being a real teacher, and I'm old enough to take care of myself."

"She won't like it."

"And I want to get a dog."

"She's *definitely* not going to like that."

"I know. That's why I'm hoping you'll help."

India felt her body tense as she imagined Boo playing soccer on the grassy field at school, or running in the park with a dog—then bent over and struggling for breath.

And she wouldn't be there to help.

For years, India had said no to parties and sleepovers—not because she didn't want to go, but because she didn't want to be away from Boo.

In case.

Those two words looked so innocent, but for the Wimple family, they meant so much.

What Boo was asking really was monumental. But India knew he was right. It was time they all let him grow up.

"I promise I'll help."

"Thank you," Boo said. "You really are the best sister in the world."

"Don't thank me yet," India said. "Because Mom is not going to like it one little bit."

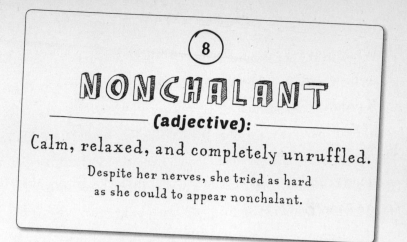

8

NONCHALANT

(adjective):

Calm, relaxed, and completely unruffled.

Despite her nerves, she tried as hard
as she could to appear nonchalant.

THE WIMPLES WERE READY. AFTER weeks of planning, practicing, and packing, they were buckled into their plane seats and settling back for their journey to London.

Dad helped Mom feel better by making absolutely sure they were fully prepared if Boo had an attack. He gave inhalers to each of the Wimples, who promised to have them on hand at all times. They recited Boo's asthma plan over breakfast until they knew it by heart, and in the evenings, Dad led spelling bees using asthma terms.

Symptoms.

Allergens.

Antihistamine.

In true Yungabilla style, the town had rallied to help India prepare for her big moment. Every day, new words appeared on storefronts and on Mrs. Rahim's front window at the hub, while Mrs. Wild held spelling bees every afternoon in class. The townsfolk gave them travel gifts they thought would be useful, like fanny packs and homemade candies. Mrs. O'Donnell and Gracie Hubbard made India a white chiffon dress with three pearl buttons down the front so she could have something special to wear to the final. They even included a pocket for her lucky hanky.

But the Wimples' favorite gift was from Daryl.

He'd secretly joined the Craft Society to learn how to knit so he could make the Wimples matching red scarves. "That way, you can find each other in a crowd and think of me cheering you on."

India threw her arms around his big, lanky body. "Thank you."

Daryl blinked back tears. "You're welcome."

India was packed and ready to go, but just before they left, she had one last thing to do.

She snuck into Dad's shed with a small present.

"What's this for?" he asked. "My birthday's months away."

"It's to remind you that you're a brilliant journalist, no matter what anyone says."

Dad tore off the paper and stared at a notebook with a

purple velvet cover. He opened his mouth before closing it tight without a word.

"You're welcome," India said, "but I want to be first to hear what you write."

"How about this as a headline: Small-town Girl Becomes International Spelling Champion?"

"And if I don't win?"

"Small-town Girl Is Champion to Proud Dad."

India laughed. "Can I ask a favor?"

"Anything."

India took a deep breath. "Boo wants Mom to calm down about his asthma."

"She just worries."

"We all worry," India said, "but Boo's tired of being treated like a little kid."

"He said that?"

India nodded. "And he wants to go back to school."

Dad sighed. "Oh boy, that's serious."

"There's something else." India bit her lip. "He wants a dog."

"It might be easier to get him to the moon."

"Please, Dad. Boo needs our help."

"He's got it, but we have to take this slowly."

"Thanks, Dad."

"Don't thank me yet. This is going to take some work."

On the day they left, there was a big send-off, and the entire town lined the streets, cheering and waving signs that read:

WE'LL BE WATCHING, INDIA!
INDIA—OUR HERO!

As Dad drove slowly past in the Wimples' battered old van, they waved at every well-wisher until they saw Daryl, who stood at the very end of Main Street, wearing a red scarf. He shouted, "See you soon, Wimples!"

"You will!" India cried, and the Wimples didn't stop waving until Daryl was a small dot on the horizon and Yungabilla had disappeared behind them in a haze of dust.

～～～

When they finally arrived in London, disheveled and tired after the long flight, they stepped into the frantic, crowded airport. Walking in a daze, they managed to find their luggage and were shuffled into lines and past customs booths before being spat out into the chaos of the airport terminal.

The Wimples huddled together like penguins in a snowstorm, which often happened when they felt overwhelmed.

Nanna Flo groaned at the sight of so many people. "What do we do now?"

"We need to find the driver." Dad wore what Mom called his "worry wrinkle."

Nanna Flo was elbowed in the head by a passing stranger. "Can we do it before—"

The crowd seemed to close in like a wave. The Wimples huddled even closer until Boo saw a tall, broad-shouldered man in a black cap holding a sign with their name on it. "Over there!"

They waved their red scarves to get his attention, and when they did, he expertly waded through the throng of passengers.

"My name is Beecham, and I'll be your driver. Welcome to Old Blighty. How are you finding England so far?"

"Busier than a bull at a rodeo," Nanna Flo said. "Can you get us out of here?"

Beecham snickered. "Certainly, madam."

He pulled a Union Jack umbrella from his jacket and opened it in front of him. "Stay close, everyone. I've done this many times before, but things can get hairy."

With the Wimples scurrying in his wake, Beecham cut a path through the crowd like an icebreaker in the Arctic and led them outside, where he stopped beside a shiny black Mercedes.

Dad stared wide-eyed. "Are you sure that's for us?"

Beecham held open the door. "Nothing but the best for our special visitors."

The Wimples climbed into the luxury car to find it lined with shelves of souvenirs.

"While you enjoy the ride, you may wish to purchase a small memento of your trip. A Tower of London snow dome, a wobbly-headed Prince Charles, or a waving Queen... She's my best seller. I've got Union Jack underwear, hankies, and a London Tower guard sitting on the toilet. You'll be surprised how many of those I sell."

In a haze of jet lag, Dad announced, "We'll take one of each! And some extras for friends at home."

"Thank you, sir. That'll make my wife very happy."

The Wimples each chose a souvenir while India stared at the city as it whooshed past. Everything suddenly felt too big. Cars and trucks rushed by, giving her the feeling of being caught in a raging river.

Dad put on his best royal voice and held his waving Queen in front of India. *"My husband and I welcome you to England."*

She couldn't help but smile. Dad could do that. Her anxiety sometimes made her feel like she were sinking, but Dad always knew how to bring her back.

He settled into the seat beside her. "When your mom and I lived in London, we promised that one day, we'd bring our kids here. Turns out, your clever spelling and Boo's resourcefulness brought *us* back."

As they drove farther into the center of London, the streets brimmed with double-decker buses and black cabs, and boats and ferries drifted on the River Thames. The Wimples pointed out palaces and cathedrals and—

"The London Eye!" Boo cried.

Their excitement lifted India even more. "I can't believe I'm really here."

"You bet your sweet patootie you're here," Nanna Flo said.

"Ladies and gentlemen," Beecham announced, "we have arrived." He turned into the driveway of the Royal Windsor

Hotel. "One of London's finest establishments and home to the Most Marvelous International Spelling Bee for fifty years."

It looked more like a castle than a hotel, with its tall, arched windows and steep, peaked roof. Rising from the center stood a regal clock tower, its face glowing like a full moon.

"Holy sheep dip," Nanna Flo said. "I never knew hotels could be this fancy."

Hotel doormen pulled their luggage from the trunk, while others scrambled to open their doors. The Wimples craned their necks to look outside. When they didn't move, Beecham poked his head between the seats and said, "This is the part where you go in."

"Thank you," India said.

"My pleasure." Beecham doffed his cap. "Good luck."

Dad paid Beecham for the souvenirs, and the Wimples slowly climbed out of the car, each of them feeling bedraggled and underdressed in a sea of elegant gowns and dinner jackets of the other guests. They huddled even closer together.

"Ready, Wimples?" Dad asked, sounding a little unsure himself.

India picked at the hem of her skirt and tried to push away the feeling that she didn't belong. A man in a tuxedo and shiny black top hat opened the door, and they carefully stepped inside.

The lobby lifted high above them like a cathedral, with

ornately carved ceilings, gold walls, and rich, red carpets. It was bustling with more tuxedoed staff, and guests milled beneath shimmering chandeliers.

The Wimples gazed at the splendor of it all, marveling that they, a small family from Yungabilla, Australia, could even *be* here. All of them except Nanna Flo, who was emptying a bowl of chocolates into her handbag. "They'll be lovely treats for later."

Two banners hung from the ceiling. One said:

WELCOME, SPELLERS,
TO THE MOST MARVELOUS
INTERNATIONAL SPELLING BEE

while the other announced:

THE ROYAL WINDSOR IS PROUD TO HOST
CRUPPS ANNUAL DOG SHOW

Mom was horrified. "No one said anything about a dog show. The hotel will be full of pet dander and allergens."

Unfortunately, at that very moment, Boo sneezed.

Mom pulled an inhaler from her purse in one quick motion. "Are you OK? Do you feel wheezy? Should we call the doctor?"

"I'm fine, thanks, Mom."

"We should stay at a different hotel." She pulled out her phone. "One with no animals."

India saw Boo's face fall and knew she had to help. "Boo will be extra careful, won't you?"

Boo nodded.

"Still"—Mom kept searching—"we can't be too careful."

Boo shot Dad a *rescue me* look.

"You'll tell us if you feel wheezy. Right?"

"Like always." Boo nodded.

Dad put his hand gently on Mom's. She looked up from her search. "OK," she said, relenting, "but I want to know the *second* you feel something's wrong."

Mom put her phone away, and Boo swapped a relieved look with Dad and India.

Everywhere around them, parents fussed over excited kids, and dogs were preened by their owners. Some pampered pooches were even pushed in baby carriages.

Beside a giant pyramid of Crupps Gourmet Dog Food, a woman tied a yellow ribbon into a girl's curly hair. The girl's body tensed as her mother gave the ribbon an extra-firm yank. "You're going to outshine everyone onstage. All that extra tutoring is going to win us that trophy."

Beside them, the owner of a poodle was adjusting a yellow ribbon in the dog's curly hair. "Who is Daddy's little champion, then?"

Nanna Flo frowned. "I can't tell who's the pet and who's the kid."

A young girl buried her head in a dictionary while a boy clung to his mother's arm, looking as if he were about to cry. "Come on." She dragged him behind her. "This will be *fun*."

Among all the hubbub, India noticed someone else—a boy standing beside an older man in a sweater that was wrinkled and buttoned incorrectly. They stood together, looking lost and overwhelmed.

India was about to wave when an ever-so-smiley man in a black suit and sky-blue silk cravat appeared through the crowd. "Welcome to the Most Marvelous International Spelling Bee." He bowed ever so slightly. "You must be the Wimples from Australia."

He was short and round with silvery-black waves of hair. Everything about him seemed to sparkle, from his eyes all the way to his polished shoes.

"I am Mr. Elwood O'Malley, the Queen's representative." He pointed proudly to the embroidered royal crest on his breast pocket. "It is a pleasure to make your acquaintance." The posh way he spoke made Nanna Flo feel like curtsying.

"I have had the privilege of working for Her Majesty for many years at the palace, but *this* year, I have been entrusted with making sure the bee runs smoothly. Rest assured that I have personally double- and triple-checked every detail to ensure the next few days of your life will be nothing less than extraordinary."

It was hard not to be swept up by Mr. O'Malley's exuberance, which created a ripple of excitement in each of the Wimples.

His eyes landed on India, as if Mr. O'Malley were being reunited with a long-lost friend. "It is especially wonderful to meet you, India Wimple. It is a remarkable skill to master the Queen's English, and you have my absolute admiration."

Being with Mr. O'Malley gave India the feeling of being in front of a warm, glowing fire.

He handed her a folder embossed with the Queen's insignia.

"In here, you will find my room number and phone details, information about the next few days, your spelling bee number, and"—his smile grew even wider—"a signed letter of welcome from the Queen herself."

India had to make sure she'd heard right. "For me?"

Mr. O'Malley beamed. "For you. There will be a special welcome for the spellers at four o'clock in the Imperial Dining

Hall, followed by a sumptuous dinner for all. Dress code: white."
He crouched down before Boo. "I had asthma as a child, so I
know it can be unsettling. If you feel unwell in the slightest, call
my number, and I will be there."

And with that, he bowed and moved away to greet more spellers.

"A letter from the Queen," Dad said. "That's never happened
to any Wimple, ever!"

While they pored over the letter, India's thoughts wandered
elsewhere. She glanced around the lobby in a way she hoped
wouldn't be obvious to the others, but Nanna Flo noticed
immediately.

"Looking for anyone special?" Nanna asked.

"No." India shook her head. "Why would I be looking for
anyone special? I was admiring the hotel. Can't a girl admire the
hotel?" India knew she was rambling.

"Of course you can." Mom swapped a knowing look with Dad.

"Especially," Nanna Flo said with a smile, "when someone
behind you is doing the same thing."

India spun around, and her heart lurched as if it momentarily
forgot how to work.

It was Rajish.

The same Rajish with his thick, dark hair and smile that
lifted right into the corners of his face. Rajish, who was kind

and funny and almost blew his chances in the Stupendously Spectacular Spelling Bee, just for her.

"He's here." India barely breathed.

"Who's here?" Dad pretended to have no idea what India was talking about.

"Rajish."

Boo joined in. "Rajish who?"

India would have answered, but Rajish waved, and her heart staggered a little more. She lifted her hand and waved back but stayed right where she was.

Nanna Flo nudged her in the shoulder. "Aren't you going to say hello?"

"Oh yeah, sure." India tried to appear as nonchalant as she could as she walked toward Rajish, and she was doing a very good job of it too, until the toe of her shoe caught on the carpet and she stumbled straight into his arms.

The Wimples were doing a terrible job of staring while trying to look like they weren't staring. They were not a family of natural actors.

"Sorry." India pushed her hair out of eyes.

"It's OK," Rajish said. "It happens a lot when I'm around girls."

"Does it really?"

"All the time. I'm thinking of buying accident insurance."

India laughed. Rajish could do this—just when she felt nervous, Rajish would smile or make a joke, and she would instantly feel better.

He crossed his arms. "But now that you're here, I have a complaint to make."

"You do?"

"Yes, a very serious one. It's about them."

India saw a portly man in a crisp suit and a woman wearing a sparkling blue sari. They entered the hotel, arm in arm.

"Because of you, my parents have been kissing—*a lot*—no matter where they are, which is really embarrassing."

Right on cue, Rajish's parents kissed.

"You see? My life has become a series of smooching nightmares, and it's all your fault."

"My fault?"

"Of course! If you hadn't been so charming last time we met, I would never have wanted to be your friend, and the huge book of spelling bee words that my dad carried everywhere wouldn't have been thrown under a bus by my mother so I could spend more time with you."

"I'm sorry about that."

"That's when the kissing began, and if you find it embarrassing, you only have yourself to blame."

"Did your dad buy another book?"

"No, he has a new plan." Rajish reached into his pocket and took out his phone. "He is still determined that I win, but he doesn't want to upset Mom. So he has made a recording of the most difficult words of the last ten years. He says if I listen to it as I fall asleep, the words will embed themselves into my subconscious."

"India!" Mrs. Kapoor swooped in and smothered her in a hug. "It is so lovely to see you again."

India enjoyed being swept up in the perfumed scent of Mrs. Kapoor's sari.

"Yes, indeed." Mr. Kapoor shook India's hand. "We are looking forward to another great battle."

Mrs. Kapoor frowned at her husband until he added, "But mostly, we are looking forward to being with old friends again." He held a finger in the air. "I am only speaking the truth."

Mrs. Kapoor linked arms with her husband. "You two catch up while we check in."

It was then that Rajish saw something out of the corner of his eye. Or more precisely, someone. "Oh no. She's here."

"Who?" India followed his stare. "Oh. She's back."

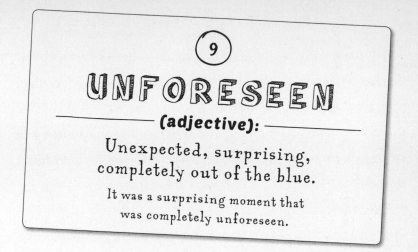

9

UNFORESEEN

(adjective):

Unexpected, surprising, completely out of the blue.

It was a surprising moment that was completely unforeseen.

THROUGH THE DOORS OF THE Royal Windsor Hotel strode Summer Millicent Ernestine Beauregard-Champion.

She moved as if she were in a shampoo commercial. Her dress shimmered, and her blond hair bounced and swished. Summer thought it was very important to make an impression every time she entered a room.

And this was no exception.

India and Rajish had met Summer during the Stupendously Spectacular Spelling Bee, and her superior attitude was disagreeable to everyone, especially India.

"Do you think she's changed?" Rajish watched as the doorman who had opened the door for her bowed.

"Maybe." India was hopeful, especially as Summer seemed to soften by the end of the bee, and they'd become *almost* friends.

Summer sailed by without saying thank you, while a young woman behind her juggled boxes and bags, hurrying to keep up.

India sighed. "Or maybe not."

Summer stopped in the center of the lobby and tucked her sunglasses on top of her luxurious hair. She scanned the room to make sure most people had seen her entrance.

When she saw India, her supremely confident pose wilted a little and was replaced by a small, hopeful smile.

"Is she smiling at us?" Rajish asked.

India nodded. "I think so."

Summer resumed her more self-assured manner and sashayed toward them.

"Rajish! India!" she cried. "It's *so* good to see you."

"It is?" India asked.

Summer threw her head back and laughed. "Of course it is. Australia's top three spellers are back, ready to take on the world!"

There was an awkward pause.

Rajish searched over her shoulder. "What have you done with the real Summer? The one who wasn't all that nice to—"

"She's gone," Summer interrupted, eager not to be reminded. "I mean, I'm here, but…" She dropped the fake smile. "I'm sorry if I was a little…*difficult* last time, but I was hoping we could start afresh."

"Start afresh?" Rajish rubbed his chin.

India followed his lead. "We'll have to think about it."

"Oh." Summer looked disappointed.

They let her linger a few seconds. "OK," Rajish decided. "I've thought about it." He flashed his sparkling smile. "That would be fine."

"Really?"

"I agree," India said. "We had a bumpy start last time, but that's no reason we can't be friends now."

"Awesome!" Summer squealed, which was something she never did, and quickly composed herself. "I mean, excellent."

Just then, something else extraordinary happened.

A man and a woman dressed in spandex tights and matching T-shirts with the words *Beaut Butts and Guts* burst into the hotel. The woman placed a speaker on the grand piano, to the horror of the piano player, and high-energy music blared as they began to perform synchronized aerobic moves.

"Are you tired of feeling fat?" the man cried. "Do you wish you could have muscles like these?" He flexed his sizeable arms. "Are you searching for the *real* you trapped beneath all that flab?"

India noticed a girl with long braids tiptoe into the hotel and slip behind a potted plant.

"Well, today is your lucky day," the woman added with

exaggerated glee, "because we here at Beaut Butts and Guts have come to help. With our specially designed exercise program, you'll have your ideal body in weeks! No butt is too big! No gut is too flabby!"

The girl briefly peeked out from behind the plant before ducking back into the foliage.

The music became faster as the woman cartwheeled away from the man. She turned and ran toward him, leaping into his arms. They announced victoriously, "We've got the butts and guts for you!"

The music came to an uplifting finish. The two stood like a weirdly composed statue. No one moved except for the girl behind the potted plant, who melted to the floor in a pool of embarrassment.

There was a strained silence until a lone person clapped.

"Thank you." The man set the woman down, and they took a bow. "We're Jenny and Terry Trifle, and we're here to help." He zeroed in on a woman eating a chocolate bar. "Ma'am, you look like you could use Beaut Butts and Guts."

They moved through the crowd, handing out business cards with broad smiles plastered on their tanned faces. The girl behind the plant cradled her head in her hands. India decided she was going to introduce herself when an unforeseen event unfolded.

It happened like this:

High above them, the rope from the canvas spelling bee banner had frayed after more than fifty years of swaying from the ceiling of the Royal Windsor Hotel. And now those frayed strands were beginning to weaken. One by one, they snapped, and the banner began to sag.

But no one noticed.

Not yet.

The weight of the sagging banner meant the strands broke

even faster until the last few finally gave way. The banner crumpled like a torn parachute and rippled toward the ground.

A handful of guests and staff looked up. Some called out. Most dove to get out of the way. Except for Terry and Jenny Trifle, who were busy talking about butts and guts. When people backed away from him, Mr. Trifle thought they were being shy or were intimidated by his biceps. He was wrong. They wanted to avoid what was most certainly going to happen next.

The grandfather who was huddled with his grandson saw it all unfolding clearly.

"Wait here," he said before running toward Nanna Flo, who was tipping a bowl of apples into her handbag, oblivious to the danger. Seconds before the heavy banner reached the ground, he scooped her out of the way.

It was then that Mr. Trifle finally looked up. His only words were "Oh no," before he and Mrs. Trifle were smothered in the many folds of the spelling bee banner.

"Help!" Mrs. Trifle was furious that their perfect entrance had been so thoroughly ruined.

Mr. O'Malley and the hotel staff were hurrying to their rescue when Nanna Flo realized she was in the arms of a stranger. And holding the empty bowl. "Thank you."

"You're welcome." The man placed her feet on the ground. "I used to be a firefighter. Acting fast in a crisis was part of the job."

Mrs. Trifle continued to screech from beneath the banner. "Get this off me!" Her arms flailed, making it harder for the hotel staff to untangle her.

"At least it put a stop to their nonsense."

"I couldn't agree more."

Nanna Flo did something she very rarely did: she giggled.

Mr. Trifle's muffled voice could be heard from beneath the banner. "I'm coming, Pumpkin."

India saw the girl with the braids slowly emerge from behind the potted plant. Her body seemed weighed down, as if she were carrying an enormous weight, and her face was a picture of pure misery.

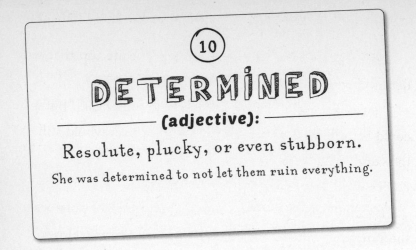

10

DETERMINED

(adjective):

Resolute, plucky, or even stubborn.

She was determined to not let them ruin everything.

IT HAD BEEN MANY MONTHS since a less confident, more anxious India had first found herself competing in the Stupendously Spectacular Spelling Bee. Back then, even the idea of being with strangers would make India break out in goose bumps and her stomach twist into a nauseous knot.

Entering the bee had helped India face her fears and, to her surprise, not feel nearly as sick. She even enjoyed it—in the end.

But standing in their suite in the Royal Windsor Hotel, about to meet the other contestants, some of those earlier feelings came back—feeling out of place, that she was just an ordinary girl from a small country town who didn't belong. It made her pulse quicken and her head spin.

"How do I look?"

India was wearing white pants with a white top that was her mother's.

"You look perfect!" Dad kissed her on the forehead. "But you could be wearing a potato sack, and my answer would still be the same."

"Thanks, Dad, but I know you're fibbing."

"It's true!" Mom said. "You dressed as a sack of potatoes at the Yungabilla Show when you were five and won first prize."

"That proves it!" Nanna Flo looked at her watch. "You better go. You don't want to be late for your meeting."

"But I don't really know how to talk to strangers."

"First thing is to smile," Mom said. "It makes everyone feel better."

"Then tell them your name and where you're from," Boo added.

"Find something you have in common," Dad said. "That always worked when I was a journalist."

"Try to make them laugh," Nanna Flo said. "People love a good laugh."

India hoped she could remember everyone's advice.

"But mostly," Mom said, "be yourself, and everyone will see how charming you are."

"You are charming," Boo agreed.

"You'll charm the pants off of them," Dad said.

"Anyone who isn't charmed is a pickle," Nanna Flo declared.

India smiled. Once again, her family had lifted her spirits just as they were about to tumble.

Until what Dad said next. "Plus, they won't all be strangers. Rajish will be there."

"Rajish?" India's heart lurched again, as if she were suddenly on a ship that had hit a huge wave.

"Yes." Dad frowned. "Your friend. Remember?"

"Of course I remember." India's overzealous laugh made the rest of the Wimples frown too. "Nanna's right. I better go."

As the Wimples waved her off and the elevator doors slid shut, India hoped she wouldn't freeze, or say anything silly, or have nothing to say at all.

Moments later, the doors opened, and a short, stout woman carrying a clipboard stepped inside. She wore all black, with a helmet of black hair and a miserable pout, as if she'd lost something precious long ago. If everything about Mr. O'Malley was smiley, everything about this woman was most definitely not.

Around her neck was a name tag that read: *Esmerelda Stomp, Most Marvelous International Spelling Bee, Director.*

India remembered the Wimples' advice, took a steadying breath, and gave it a shot.

She offered a smile but immediately worried that it came out more as a grimace, so she tried the next step: the introduction. "I'm India Wimple from Australia."

Esmerelda, who was focused on her clipboard, offered a small grunt.

India tried the next step: she needed to find something they had in common.

"It must be a dream job working on a competition that inspires children all over the world."

Esmerelda slowly turned to India. Her stare was so cold that the temperature in the elevator seemed to drop. "Listen, kid, don't take this the wrong way, but I don't like spelling bees or children. I fell into this job when the previous director went on vacation and never came back. I'm not sure why I didn't do the same." Esmerelda's face was chiseled with a seriousness that made India wonder if she'd ever smiled in her life. "In fact, I wouldn't mind if the bee were canceled. No more pushy brats with their even pushier parents thinking their kids are the bee's knees. No more tantrums or tears when they lose, and no more runaway egos when they win. Gives me indigestion just thinking about it."

"Spelling bees can be very stressful."

"Stressful? When I was a kid, you almost had to lose a limb before adults paid you any attention, and even then, you weren't allowed to cry."

"That seems kind of cruel," India said.

"Toughened us up. Prepared us for all the rotten things that would happen in life." Esmerelda raised an eyebrow. "And the rotten jobs we'd be stuck with."

She glanced up as if she were staring out an imaginary window. "I should have been a pig farmer, like I planned. Cute snouts and curly tails. Spelling bee director? A dream job? *Pah!*"

Ping!

The doors opened, and Esmerelda stomped out without another word, leaving India with the feeling that she'd been dropped into a pile of snow. She hadn't even gotten to the part about trying to make the woman laugh. She rubbed her arms to warm them up and stepped into the busy lobby, which was bubbling with music and the excited murmurings and laughter of its guests.

Ping!

Another elevator opened beside her, and the Trifles swaggered out in matching black sweat suits and fluorescent yellow sneakers. The young girl with braids crept out behind them.

Mr. Trifle was munching on a strip of beef jerky. "This spelling bee thingamabob is very impressive." He surveyed the packed lobby with a satisfied grin.

"Yes," Mrs. Trifle said. "We're very proud of you, Molly."

Holly looked over her shoulder in case her mom really was talking to someone called Molly. "Me?"

"Of course! Look at all these people hoping their kid is going to win, when we know it's going to be you."

Holly smiled. Her mom had never once said anything nice thing to her, but here she was, telling her she was *proud*.

Maybe being at the Most Marvelous International Spelling Bee would bring them closer together after all. Maybe she could prove to them that, even though she wasn't like Gertrude and

Benedict, they were still a family, and that was something to be cherished. Those were the kinds of endings that often happened in the books she'd read.

Maybe it was going to happen to her too.

Mrs. Trifle rubbed her hands together. "Not only will you collect that prize money, but the publicity is going to bring in a flood of new customers. We're going to make a very tidy profit for Beaut Butts and Guts."

"What?" Holly didn't even try to hide her disappointment.

"This place is a gold mine." Mrs. Trifle flung her arm across the room. "Just look at all these sagging arms and flabby bellies."

"The poor level of fitness is magnificent," Mr. Trifle beamed. "We're going to make a killing."

Holly worried that she was about to be sick all over her parents' sweat suits and brand-new sneakers.

"But most of the spellers are from overseas," Holly argued. "They won't want to sign up to a gym in Canada."

"It's *not* a gym, Molly," Mrs. Trifle snapped. "It's a fitness and beauty lifestyle, which will one day be worldwide, but until then, people can sign up for online classes and buy our stylish workout clothes, personalized squat routines, and a wide range of healthy snacks."

Mr. Trifle waved his beef jerky, which Holly thought smelled like an old leather shoe. "Like the Beaut Butts and Guts Protein-Packed Jerky, made from the finest strips of beef and dried to perfection. Who can resist that?" He threw the remaining piece in his mouth. "*Mmm-mmm*. De-licious," he mumbled. "And you brought us here, sweetheart, and made it all possible."

Holly was regretting that fact with each passing moment.

She stared at her parents, who were wide-eyed with glee at the prospect of so much money within tantalizing reach. Her whole body sank in misery.

"Stand up straight," Mrs. Trifle ordered. "Why do you slouch all the time? It's like you're trying to hide from something."

Holly did as she was told, even though hiding from her family sounded like the perfect idea.

"You're a Trifle, and that's something to be proud of," Mrs. Trifle said. "Especially when you look around this room. Look at all these out-of-shape, roly-poly porkers just crying out for our help."

Holly's skin prickled with fear. She hoped no one could hear what her parents were saying.

Mrs. Trifle took a stack of business cards from her fanny pack.

"Please." Holly tried to stop her. "Maybe this isn't a good time."

"Ah, but you see, Molly, that's where you're wrong," Mrs. Trifle said. "That's why we're the parents and you're the child. This is the *perfect* time. As people stuff a cream puff or hot dog in their mouths, we'll innocently walk up beside them and make them feel so guilty that they'll immediately sign up for our classes."

And as it happened so many times in Holly's life, just as she thought her parents couldn't get any more embarrassing, her mother began doing jumping jacks.

"Go and play with the other children," she ordered. "You might even make a friend."

"A friend?" Holly asked.

"Yes, a friend," her mother said. "But focus on the pudgy ones so you can drum up business." She stopped her jumping jacks and turned to Mr. Trifle. "Ready, darling?"

"Ready." He kissed his daughter on the head. "Have fun."

As they strode headlong into the crowd, Holly remembered: "Don't forget to wear white." Holly wasn't very tall anyway, but being with her parents often made her feel even smaller. She wanted to slink away to her hotel room and was about to get back in the elevator when she heard a voice behind her.

It was India. "Are you OK?"

Holly nodded as she watched her parents approach another victim. "They mean well. They can just be a little…" she struggled to find the right word, "…*fixated*, sometimes."

The room buzzed with people and pooches from the bee and

the dog show, laughing and barking. Holly stood in the middle of it all as if she was lost.

India knew exactly how that felt.

This time, she was *determined* to make her family's friendship advice work.

She smiled. "I'm India, from Australia."

"I'm Holly, from Canada."

It's going well so far, India thought. *Now I need to find something that we have in common.*

"It's strange, isn't it? How being here can be so exciting and yet so terrifying at the same time?"

Holly's eyes widened. "You feel that too?"

"Most of the time, I waver between wanting to laugh and wanting to throw up."

Holly laughed. "I thought it was just me."

It worked, India thought. *The Wimple friendship advice worked.* "Do you want to go in together?"

"Yes, please."

And just like that, Holly Trifle and India Wimple both made a new friend, and they entered the Imperial Dining Hall for the opening of the Most Marvelous International Spelling Bee.

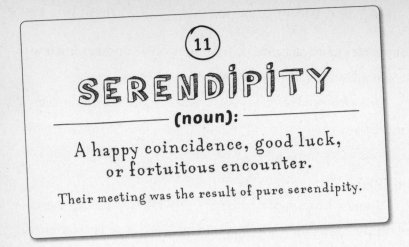

SERENDIPITY

(noun):

A happy coincidence, good luck, or fortuitous encounter.

Their meeting was the result of pure serendipity.

WALKING INTO THE IMPERIAL DINING Hall erased any unpleasantness Holly and India had just experienced. Hundreds of lights dangled from the roof and were fashioned into the shape of letters, while the walls were lit with moving words of all sizes, revolving over the surface like a mirror ball, giving the effect of being inside the pages of a glowing, oversize dictionary.

Wondrous.

Extraordinary.

Fantabulous.

Holly and India burst into giddy smiles.

In the center of the hall, rows of banquet tables shimmered with candles, and bouquets of white letters bloomed from vases, but what caught India's and Holly's attention next were the tables of crystal cake stands piled with cupcakes, each with a chocolate letter nestled on swirls of colorful icing.

Holly felt her knees weaken. "Mom and Dad would never let me eat any of this."

"Yes," said India with a knowing grin, "but they're not here, are they?"

"I guess one wouldn't hurt." Holly chose a plump cupcake with pink, creamy icing topped with the letter H. Her cheeks bulged after her first mouthful, and she smiled in delight.

"It'll be our secret." India bit into her own.

"Oh no." Beside them, a boy stared down at his shirt, which was now covered in splotches of ruby-red icing. "This often happens," he explained. "It's like food jumps out at me, no matter how careful I am."

India handed him a napkin, but it only spread the mess farther across his chest. "Oh dear."

"Does anyone know if these letters are Belgian chocolate?"

It was Summer. Of course.

"I only eat Belgian chocolate." She noticed the boy's stained shirt and stepped back in case her brand-new dress was smudged too.

"I had a small accident." The boy wanted to get rid of the look of horror on Summer's face. "I'm Peter," he said as he held out his hand, until he remembered it was also smeared with icing.

Rajish ran in, puffing. "Oh good. It hasn't started."

"Where have you been?" India asked.

"Mom went to the art gallery, so Dad decided to cram in some spelling practice. I only just got away."

India thought she saw something move beneath Peter's jacket. Growing up in the country, creatures sometimes crept into unexpected places. The Wimples had found snakes in closets, mice in shoes, and spiders under the toilet seat, so she said calmly, "I don't want to worry you, but I think there might be an animal in your pocket."

Peter smiled. "That's Prince Harry." He opened his jacket, and out poked the head of what looked like a miniature dragon with feathery yellow spines running down his back and head. "He's my crested gecko, loyal friend, and fellow traveler. He's trying to tell me it's dinnertime."

Peter took a cricket from his other pocket and fed it to Prince Harry.

Summer wasn't sure what horrified her the most—the reptile or the fact that she'd just seen it eat a bug. "You brought a lizard to the spelling bee?"

"He's very tame." Peter held him out. "You can pat him if you like."

Summer reeled back. "No, thanks."

"Can I?" Holly and India both asked.

"Me too," Rajish said.

Prince Harry arched his back, enjoying all the attention.

"They were discovered in New Caledonia in 1866 and were thought to be extinct until they were found again in 1994," Peter said.

"My dear champion spellers," Mr. O'Malley announced, beaming like a beacon of happiness at the front of the room. "It is time to begin." He stood in front of a grand fireplace and beneath a portrait of the Queen.

Peter slipped Prince Harry back into his pocket.

"As you know, I am Mr. Elwood O'Malley, the Queen's

royal representative for the Most Marvelous International Spelling Bee."

There was a spontaneous round of applause.

"It is one of the greatest honors of my life to be here on behalf of Her Majesty and to be in the company of the world's masterful spellers. You are about to experience some of the most remarkable days of your life. The competition will provide moments of exhilaration and apprehension and will create new and treasured friendships and memories that will linger in your hearts forever."

Mr. O'Malley's effervescence washed over the room. It swept India up in a wave of excitement, while Holly clung to every word.

Mr. O'Malley took a hanky from his pocket and dabbed his eyes.

"Is he crying?" Summer frowned.

"I think so," India said.

"But before that," he sniffed, "it is imperative that you become acquainted with one another. Please turn to the people closest to you and take three minutes each to share a little about yourself, including your favorite word. The person nearest to me will begin." Mr. O'Malley gave the groups time to form and held up his watch. "Your time starts now."

Summer swished her blond locks over her shoulders. "My name is Summer Millicent Ern–"

"Actually, Summer," India interrupted, "Peter is first."

"Oh." Summer was a little miffed. "OK."

"My name is Peter," he began shakily, "but most people call me Chubby. I'm ten and live in Wormwood, England, with my mom and grandpop. My dad left a few months after I was born, but I've always thought if he'd stuck around a little longer, he might have found I was fun to be with." He laughed nervously. "I was being picked on at school until Mrs. Wrenshaw, the librarian, thought going to the library at lunchtime might help, but I said, 'No offense, I wouldn't be seen dead in the library.' She told me to come anyway, and I'm glad I did. There was this whole world of books and reading I'd never known before. That's why I love words so much—they rescued me from being bullied, and now they're the reason I'm here, meeting all of you."

He paused. The others stared, not knowing what to say.

"Sorry, I've said too much, haven't I?" Peter's head fell, looking as if he'd just failed a test. "It's like I have a permanent case of logorrhea."

Holly hadn't heard of the word before but knew *logos* meant "word" and *rhea* meant "flow." "Talking too much?" she asked.

Peter nodded. "It happens when I'm nervous."

"It's nice to meet you, Peter," India said.

"It is?" No one had ever told him that before.

"Absolutely," Holly said. "Words rescued me too. Gave me somewhere to escape from my parents."

"But you haven't told us your favorite word, Peter," Rajish added.

Peter thought hard. "*Borborygmus.* It's the rumbling sound that comes from an empty stomach. I also get hungry when I'm nervous."

"I like *gremlin,*" Rajish said, "which is what Roald Dahl called the small creatures he thought were messing with the planes he flew during the war."

"My favorite Dahl word is *biffsquiggled,*" Summer added, "which he uses when the BFG feels confused."

"I get biffsquiggled quite a lot," Peter admitted.

"I like *serendipity,*" India said.

"I love *kerfuffle* and *rumpus* and *bafflegab,*" Holly said.

"I also like *flibbertigibbet,*" Peter said. "*Onomatopoeia* and *triskaidekaphobia,* which is fear of the number thirteen."

"Who would be scared of a number?" Summer asked.

"People who have triskaidekaphobia," Peter answered with a knowing grin.

They all laughed at once, like they were thinking the same thing. And that made them laugh even more.

Peter felt braver. It was the first time ever that he was surrounded by a group of children who weren't laughing at him but with him.

And he liked it.

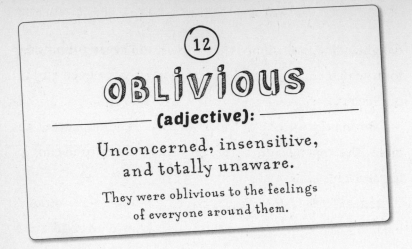

12

OBLIVIOUS

(adjective):

Unconcerned, insensitive,
and totally unaware.

They were oblivious to the feelings
of everyone around them.

"AND THAT'S HOW DARYL SAVED a busload of schoolkids from being swept into the floodwaters of the Yungabilla Creek."

Dinner had been served in the Imperial Dining Hall, and Dad had been telling stories he'd written when he was a journalist.

"That was very exciting, Mr. Wimple." Mrs. Kapoor was especially impressed. "You have a real talent for storytelling."

"She is only speaking the truth!" Mr. Kapoor was equally impressed.

"He's one of the best," India said.

"Can you tell us another story?" Peter asked.

Dad was about to launch into one more when he was interrupted by the Trifles. Still wearing their black sweat suits and bright yellow sneakers, they stood out like seals in a pod of pelicans.

"Ah, there you are, Molly." Mrs. Trifle sat beside her

daughter. She took off one of her shoes and began rubbing her foot, which she'd plonked on the table. "We've been run off our feet today."

"But it was worth it." Mr. Trifle said, heading toward the table. "We've signed up lots of new recruits. They're all chomping at the bit to have new butts and guts."

A team of waiters approached the table, all expertly balancing plates of food. One waiter leaned over to serve them. "Chicken Kiev with roast potatoes and gravy or pasta Napoletana with parmesan?"

Mrs. Trifle waved him off. "Heavens no! Are you trying to harden my arteries? I'd like poached chicken with quinoa and Asian greens. Pronto. I'm starving."

If the waiter was annoyed by Mrs. Trifle's rudeness, he never let it show. "And for you, sir?"

Mr. Trifle opened his mouth, but Mrs. Trifle answered for him. "He'll have the same, won't you, dear?"

Mr. Trifle stared at the plates of chicken Kiev and pasta as they sailed away from him and were placed in front of the others. "Yes, of course."

Holly whispered to her mother, "So that means you can relax now and stop handing out—"

"We're going to make a killing with these people." It seemed as if Mrs. Trifle hadn't even noticed Holly'd begun talking.

Holly desperately needed them to change the subject. "These are my new friends," she blurted out. "And their families."

"Friends? *Really?*" Even though Mrs. Trifle had suggested that her daughter make a friend, she was surprised it had actually happened.

Holly looked around nervously, wondering if she'd spoken too soon.

"Yes, we are friends," India declared. "My name is India, and this is Summer, Rajish, and—"

"Chubby." Mrs. Trifle's eyes landed on Peter.

"No." Holly wore an anxious smile. "His name is Peter."

Mrs. Trifle slipped her shoe back on, took her foot off the table, and affected an air of concern. "Do other kids tease you about being chubby?"

The entire table stopped eating, and Holly felt as if a small part inside her was actually breaking. "Mom, I don't think Peter wants to…"

Mr. and Mrs. Trifle didn't hear Holly's protests. Instead, they leaned in like lions creeping up on a small, defenseless animal.

"Don't you dream of being like the other kids?" Mr. Trifle asked.

Peter stopped eating his chicken Kiev. His grandfather gave him a small look to see if he was OK.

Holly wished the floor would open up and swallow her parents whole, but luckily, it didn't have to, because India's dad got in first.

"We're the Wimples. These are the Kapoors and Mr. Eriksson, Peter's grandfather."

"It's a pleasure to meet you," Mrs. Trifle said, sounding like she didn't mean a word of it.

Holly turned to Peter. "I'm sorry."

Peter pushed his barely touched meal away. His hands clenched into a tight ball in his lap. "It doesn't matter." He waved a hand, trying to be as convincing as possible.

But Holly could see that it did matter. It mattered very much.

Suddenly, a waiter pouring water accidentally spilled some on Mrs. Trifle's sweat suit.

"You imbecile!" Mrs. Trifle dabbed her suit with a napkin. "Look what you've done! I'm soaked!"

He offered her the napkin from his arm, but she waved him away. "I'm so sorry, madam."

India thought the waiter didn't look very sorry at all. In fact, she saw the smallest smidgeon of a smile as he moved to serve another table.

"Mr. Wimple was telling us stories about when he was young." Mr. Kapoor hoped to get the attention off the Trifles.

"I've got a story." Mr. Trifle sat back in her chair. "I remember when I won the Bognor Regis Triathlon. Came in first, beating all the younger competitors."

"You were marvelous that day, my dear." Mrs. Trifle laid a hand on her husband's arm. "In fact, that is when I fell in love with him. He was holding the trophy, being applauded by thousands, and I knew he'd be the perfect partner—in marriage and in business."

Mrs. Trifle stared pointedly at Peter, who had lowered his head and seemed not to be listening to a word. "You could be strong and lean one day, Peter."

Peter glanced up. "Sorry?"

"My grandson is fine the way he is." Grandpop put a protective hand on Peter's shoulder.

"Yes, but we can all *improve*." Mrs. Trifle was miffed that she had to state the painfully obvious.

"Absolutely." Mr. Trifle rolled up his sleeve and flexed. "You could have muscles like these."

Holly wished it was just a bad dream and not her *actual* father showing his *actual* muscles during dinner.

"They are...prodigious," Peter said.

Mr. and Mrs. Trifle swapped puzzled looks. Having never heard the word before, they wondered if it was a compliment or if Peter didn't understand how enormous they really were.

Holly was in agony. Why did she even come? It wasn't even that her parents were *trying* to embarrass her. It just came naturally to them.

"Hard work, that's what it is." Thankfully, Mr. Trifle rolled down his sleeve. "You don't get guns like this without a lot of effort."

"Yes, sir," Peter barely mumbled.

"A boy your age should be looking after his health and keeping fit. You want to be a hit with the ladies, right?"

"Codswallop!" Nanna Flo dropped her knife and fork with a

great clatter. It was safe to say she'd had enough. "What you *look* like has absolutely diddly-squat to do with *who* you are and why someone might like you."

A smile slithered onto Mrs. Trifle's lips, a look that could only be described as condescending. It took all of Nanna Flo's resolve not to tip more water over her.

"And you are…?"

"Florence Wimple."

"Florence, I don't mean to be rude—"

"Really? Because you're just about the rudest person I've ever met. We're here to celebrate these kids, and all you've done is criticize them and talk about yourselves. And I, for one, have had a gutful."

There was a brief, awkward silence where no one knew what to say next, until Grandpop Eriksson spoke up.

"Florence is right," he said. "These kids deserve our support. You two would benefit from working on your manners as well as your muscles."

Peter was impressed. He'd never heard Grandpop say anything he thought would make a fuss.

Mrs. Kapoor patted her husband's portly belly. "Even those of us who aren't athletes are most definitely adorable." She landed a particularly loud kiss on her husband's cheek.

Mrs. Trifle wasn't quite sure how she and her husband could be telling the truth and yet have everyone at the table disagree with them. "If young children can learn from what we've achieved in our lives, then it's a crime for us not to impart our wisdom."

"Wisdom?" Nanna Flo said as she stabbed at a crispy roast potato with her fork. "I'd call it a steaming pile of poppycock!"

India and Boo snuffled back their giggles. Mom and Dad couldn't help it either, which set off the Erikssons and the Kapoors, until a ripple of chuckles spread around the table.

Mrs. Trifle stood firm. "That may be what they think in New Zealand, but in Canada, we believe that—"

"We're from Australia," Boo said.

Mrs. Trifle shivered as if someone had dropped cold water on her—again. "*Australia?* I don't know how you can live there— all those spiders, snakes, and sharks… The place is crawling with animals that can kill you. You wouldn't get me there for all the tea in India."

"India?" Mr. Trifle scoffed. "Wouldn't catch me there either—curry gives me the runs."

"I'll tell you something else that gives me the runs…" Nanna Flo mumbled.

Mr. Kapoor held a finger in the air. "India is a very fine

nation. It is the cradle of the human race, the birthplace of language, the—"

"In fact," Mr. Trifle continued, oblivious to how offensive he was being, "a friend of mine was so sick after traveling to India that he was on the toilet for—"

"Ladies, gentlemen, and spelling champions." Mr. O'Malley thankfully saved them from any more of Mr. Trifle's unfortunate toilet story. "Welcome to the official opening of the Most Marvelous International Spelling Bee."

The crowd burst into fevered applause, everyone except for Holly, who looked as she did when India first saw her: small, alone, and terribly miserable.

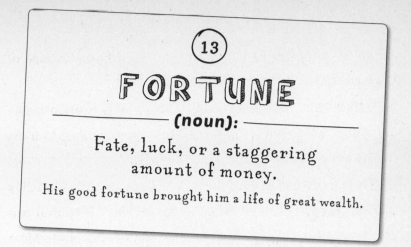

13

FORTUNE

——— (noun): ———

Fate, luck, or a staggering
amount of money.

His good fortune brought him a life of great wealth.

"CONGRATULATIONS ON BEING CHOSEN FOR the world's most prestigious spelling competition." Mr. O'Malley's face radiated a rosy glow as his words flowed through the hall. "You are the crème de la crème of spelling aficionados, and of that, you should be exceedingly proud."

This time, there was no stopping the cheers and whistling as proud adults applauded and kids wriggled in their seats with excitement.

"Before the bee commences, we have a few surprises in store, including a splendacious treat tomorrow that will enchant and amaze." Mr. O'Malley paused for effect. "And may even change your life."

He let the moment hang in the air like a colorful piñata.

They watched as Mr. Smiley O'Malley again dabbed his eyes.

"But for now, it is with the utmost delight that I introduce your spelling bee director, Ms. Esmerelda Stomp."

There was more applause as India watched the glum woman from the elevator lumber to the microphone.

Esmerelda sighed at the overexcited faces, gleaming with delight, as if there were no place they'd rather be.

Well, she could think of plenty of places *she'd* rather be.

"All right, quiet down, or we'll never get this over with."

The crowd fell silent.

"Over the next few days, you spellers will compete in two knockout rounds, which means you'll only have one chance to spell each word correctly, and if you blow that"—she jabbed a thumb at the air—"you're gone."

Esmerelda smiled for the first time since taking the microphone.

"The pronouncer's decision is final. I don't want any tears, sulking, or hissy fits." She pointed a stubby finger at the crowd. "That goes for you grown-ups too. I won't stand for any molly-coddling nonsense—turns kids into marshmallows. What good are they then?"

The audience shifted awkwardly in their seats, except Mrs. Trifle, who thought Esmerelda was making perfect sense.

"If your child fizzles out, adults are to applaud as they exit the stage." She paused and threw her glare around the room like a beam from a lighthouse, making sure her rules sunk in. "Round one will continue until half the spellers are eliminated. Round two is the grand final and will continue until we have eradicated everyone and only the winner remains."

Esmerelda's speech felt more like instructions for a hunting expedition than a children's spelling bee.

She leaned into the microphone, which made her voice boom even more ominously throughout the room. "Any questions?"

Her menacing stare unnerved the crowd enough that there were none.

"Now that we understand each other, it's time to hand this over to the next speaker. He's the *only* three-time winner of the Most Marvelous International Spelling Bee, and he's here for a pep talk, so listen up! I give you…Harrington Hathaway the Third."

Esmerelda shuffled away. If she was all gloom, Harrington was all elegance and optimism, with his silver mane and tanned face. His cape billowed out as he swooped to the microphone, waving his diamond-encrusted cane at the adoring audience.

"Bravo!" Mr. Kapoor jumped to his feet. "Bravo!"

"My dad's a big fan," Rajish said to India. "He wants me to be just like him."

"Please." Harrington held up his hand. "Don't expire yourselves before the spelling bee even begins."

The crowd laughed. Harrington soaked in the adoration.

"It is with multitudinous thanks that I greet you tonight. You have battled valiantly and spelled magnificently to make it here. But"—he paused, gazing into the audience with a warning eye—"one small slipup could end it all. It will be nerve-racking. It will be discomposing. It will be discountenancing, but great fortitude always triumphs over great adversity."

Harrington stood back, closed his eyes for a moment, and relished the applause.

"For many people, spelling may not seem important, but you and I know better. It makes us rich in mind and heart." He held his bejeweled fingers against his jacket. "It has also given me a fortunate life, and tonight, I would like to share that good fortune with you."

He smiled a Cheshire cat grin.

"If you look under your seat, you will find a small gift."

The diners bent down to retrieve packages that were taped to the bottom of their chairs. A flurry of unwrapping followed.

"A book." Mrs. Trifle's lip turned down in disappointment. "I was hoping it would be something useful."

"It's a copy of my new publication, *Being Harrington Hathaway the Third: From Humble Beginnings to Global Spelling Guru.* But that's not all," Harrington said. "Inside, you will find a small treat."

A wave of gasps swept through the room. India opened her book to find a silver hook bookmark with a sparkling gem dangling from the end.

"Is it a real diamond?" Mrs. Trifle asked.

Summer held it up against the glow of a candle. "It looks real."

"And yes," Harrington said, raising a silver eyebrow, "the diamonds are real."

The audience rose to their feet, wild with appreciation. If Harrington wasn't sure everyone in the audience loved him, he was certain of it now.

"Please." Harrington held up a silencing hand. "It is merely a token of my admiration for your brilliance. I would like to declare the Most Marvelous International Spelling Bee officially launched. Now go forth and spell!"

The combination of cheers and diamonds and words circling on the walls created a joyous, dizzying effect.

Mr. O'Malley clasped his hands before him and bounced on the heels of his polished shoes. He surveyed the sea of happy faces.

The night was going perfectly. Until what happened next…

India saw a flash of ginger fur disappear beneath their table.

"Did you see that?" she asked Rajish.

"I think so. It looked like—"

Rajish was interrupted by a series of barks and growls.

And a full-bodied scream.

This came from Harrington Hathaway the Third. A stampeding Great Dane had galloped into the Imperial Dining Hall in pursuit of the ginger cat, followed by a large woman in a gold sequined dress and feathery headpiece, thundering closely behind.

"Mergatrude!" she wailed. "Come back to Mommy, darling!"

There were loud cries as more dogs entered the room. The floor was alive with fluffy, curly-haired canines in ribbons and bows—dachshunds, beagles, and pugs. They leaped onto tables and sent glasses crashing to the floor. Plates were overturned, splashing pasta sauce onto expensive white dresses and suits and hurling chicken Kievs into surprised faces.

"Someone get that cat!" Harrington screeched.

Mr. O'Malley joined the waiters, who tried to catch the escaping feline, which sidestepped them at every turn, darting between diners' legs and jumping onto laps.

"My dress!" Summer lifted her skirt. "It's Armani!"

Nanna Flo and Mom held onto Boo while Dad and Grandpop Eriksson formed a circle with the other adults, shielding the kids.

Dog owners poured into the room, hurrying after their manicured pets now drenched in gravy and tangled in strings of spaghetti and snuffling down chicken and vegetables. The stands of cupcakes were toppled, and frantic guests slipped in the slick icing mess.

The cries of pet names added to the chaos.

Fluffy!

Poochikins!

Captain Cutie-pie!

The hall was full of tail-wagging, feasting dogs.

The cat continued to run.

"Mergatrude! Come back!"

But Mergatrude didn't come back. Instead, he bounded toward the cat, which had dashed between the legs of Harrington Hathaway the Third.

Mr. O'Malley watched in horror as the Great Dane headed directly for the three-time world champion.

"Oh no," was all he could utter before the full force of the dog slammed into Harrington's chest, sending him flying through the air and crashing to the ground with a great thud.

Mr. O'Malley rushed to his side. "Mr. Hathaway! Are you OK?"

"Of course I'm not OK, you fool!" Harrington screeched and held his back. "Apart from being in terrible pain, I could have been killed!"

India watched Harrington writhe on the floor. Mr. O'Malley's face was a portrait of devastation as he helped the gentleman sit up and handed him his cane, which was now broken in two.

Harrington, it was safe to say, was more than a little peeved.

He snatched the cane from Mr. O'Malley's grip and jabbed a threatening finger into the royal representative's chest. His face twisted with rage as he hurled abuse.

India saw Mr. O'Malley flinch with each jab.

The Imperial Dining Hall lay in ruins, as if a tornado had swept through the once elegant affair. Tables and chairs were scattered across the floor, silk curtains were in tatters, guests were smeared with food, and pooches licked the now empty plates.

It was then that India noticed something curious.

Esmerelda Stomp stood at the side of the hall with her arms crossed, not bothering to help one bit, which in itself wasn't surprising.

What surprised India most was the smile on Esmerelda's face.

A smile that could only be called…gleeful.

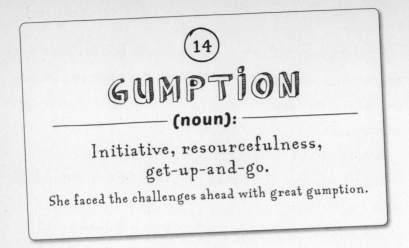

14

GUMPTION

(noun):

Initiative, resourcefulness,
get-up-and-go.

She faced the challenges ahead with great gumption.

"ONCE AGAIN, I APOLOGIZE PROFUSELY for last night's dinner, which took such an *unfortunate* turn."

The next morning, Mr. Elwood O'Malley addressed the spellers and their families, who assembled in the lobby of the Royal Windsor Hotel.

His eyes were heavy and bloodshot, as if he'd barely slept.

"I will do my utmost to ensure the Most Marvelous International Spelling Bee runs flawlessly from this moment on, and I hope that the splendidness of today's surprise will more than make up for any unpleasantness. Please, follow me."

He headed to a line of red double-decker buses waiting to take them to a secret destination.

"Are you sure you're feeling OK?" It was the fifth time Mom had asked Boo that morning.

After the dogs had run riot at the dinner, Boo had begun to wheeze and could feel his chest tighten, so the Wimples rushed him back to their room and sat with him while Mom gave him his medication.

Just in case.

Within minutes, Boo had felt better, but that didn't stop Mom from worrying.

"I'm fine." He hoped his voice didn't sound too wheezy.

She stared at her phone. "The pollution reading is high. Maybe Boo and I should stay here."

Boo had missed out on a lot of excursions because of his asthma; he didn't want to miss out on today. Luckily, Dad came to the rescue.

"Team Wimple," he said, assuming the voice of an army captain, "do we have our inhalers?"

Nanna Flo, India, and Boo whipped inhalers from their bags.

"Yes, we do," they chorused.

"Will we be prepared in the event of an asthma attack?"

"Yes, we will."

"Does Mom need to worry?"

"No, she doesn't."

Dad gently took Mom's phone and dropped it in her purse. "We'll be here if Boo needs us. OK?"

"OK, but I want you to stay with us at all times."

Dad adjusted his checkered jacket and matching tie—gifts from Mr. Butler, who he'd rescued from an angry emu. In his pocket was his purple notebook. "We better hurry, or we'll miss that bus. Ready, Wimples?"

They all wore their Sunday best and, of course, their red scarves. "Ready!"

Before they could move, they heard someone cry, "Florence!"

They turned to see Mr. Eriksson leading Peter through the crowd, waving. "Florence," he puffed. "Thank you for what you said last night at dinner. And for standing up for my grandson."

"You're welcome. I'd have done it for anyone at the mercy of those two fitness fanatics. Plus," she said as she flashed a knowing smile, "I enjoyed it."

Mr. Eriksson smiled back. "Then it was doubly worthwhile if it made you happy too."

"Oh, it did! And thank you for the fireman's rescue. That heavy banner could have done some damage. I've never been swept into someone's arms and out of great peril before."

Mr. Eriksson bowed his head. "All part of the service."

Then Nanna Flo did something the Wimples had never seen her do.

She giggled.

"All aboard!" The driver called.

Mr. Eriksson held out his hand to Nanna Flo. "After you."

"Why thank you." She giggled again as she boarded the bus.

"What's wrong with Nanna Flo?" Boo asked India. "Why does she keep laughing like that?"

"I'm not sure," India said.

"She might be coming down with something," Dad said. "We should keep an eye on her."

"Could be the jet lag," Mom added.

They climbed aboard the bus, and they heard Nanna Flo giggle once more as she moved down the aisle.

~~~~~

"The Houses of Parliament!" Boo almost jumped out of his seat when the golden clock tower and regal building came into view.

Cameras and phones clicked as the chimes of Big Ben sounded and the buses trundled across Westminster Bridge and over the River Thames.

They drove alongside the lush trees and lawns of St. James's Park and turned into a large roundabout. Little by little, a stately mansion appeared before them.

India drew in a deep breath. "Buckingham Palace!"

"Do you think we'll meet the Queen?" Boo asked.

"She is the patron of the bee and a keen speller," Rajish said hopefully.

Holly's head began to spin. "I think I might pass out."

"But you'll miss all the fun." Peter nudged her playfully.

"The Queen," Mr. Kapoor said with a wistful look in his eye. "She is a beacon of style and grace."

"If I'd known we were coming here, I'd have worn my tiara," Peter joked.

They all laughed, except for Summer, who announced with a disappointed scowl, "Me too. Why did they have to keep it a surprise?"

All the spellers stared, wondering if Summer was joking too.

"You have a tiara?" India asked.

"Daddy bought me one for my tenth birthday."

"A real one?" Holly asked.

"Is there any other kind worth having?"

"I guess not." Rajish laughed.

The buses came to a stop by the entrance gates. Streams of spellers and chaperones stepped from the buses in quiet awe.

"She's a beauty." Dad held up his camera and took photos. "Wait till Daryl hears about this."

"Your grandma would have loved this," Grandpop Eriksson said. "She was a big fan of the Queen—collected all the royal souvenir cups and plates."

"Maybe she'll give us all one for free," Mrs. Trifle said. "I bet that'll be worth a pretty penny."

Holly flinched. In her excitement, she had almost forgotten her parents were there. So far this morning, they hadn't done anything to embarrass her, and she silently pleaded that they wouldn't. At least they'd worn a dress and jacket as requested and not one of their signature sweat suits.

When the last of the passengers climbed off the bus,

Mr. O'Malley swung his arm into the air and announced, "Welcome to Buckingham Palace." He seemed to stand taller and was much more like his old, cheerful self. "Home of Her Majesty, the longest reigning monarch in British history. This way, please."

The Wimples adjusted their red scarves and followed Mr. O'Malley across the grounds to the Grand Entrance.

As India's feet sank into the royal red carpet of the Grand Hall, a quiet hush settled on the group. Walking up the Grand Staircase, she slid her hand along the banister to make sure she was really there.

"Buckingham Palace has been the official London residence of Britain's monarchs since 1837. It is simply one of the most beautiful buildings you'll ever behold."

"It is impressive." Dad took out his purple notebook and began to write.

"It boasts seven hundred and seventy-five rooms, including seventy-eight bathrooms." Mr. O'Malley smiled. "So if you need to avail yourselves of the amenities, there are plenty to accommodate. As well as the Throne Room and private quarters, there's a post office, police station, doctor's office, cinema, and pool." He continued his way through a series of drawing rooms. "Over eight hundred members of staff live here, including a flagman, a fendersmith, who looks after the palace fireplaces, and even our very own clockmaker."

"That's more people than Yungabilla," Boo said.

"Every year, the Queen hosts special parties at the palace to recognize and reward public service." Mr. O'Malley turned to face them with a look of pure delight. "And today, she is throwing a party just for you."

"For us?" Holly's eyes widened.

"Does that mean we're going to meet the Queen?" India almost dared not ask.

Mr. O'Malley paused for the smallest of moments. "It most certainly does."

"Did you hear that, Peter?" Grandpop Eriksson had a spark in his voice that Peter hadn't heard in a very long time. "The Queen is coming *here* to meet *us*."

Mr. Kapoor grabbed his chest. "I think my heart is in danger of exploding with joy."

Mr. O'Malley flung open a set of doors. "This is the White Drawing Room, the grandest of all the State Rooms."

The room was the color of honeycomb and filled with golden furniture, gold filigree on the walls, and even a gold piano. In the center was a long table laid with trays of perfectly portioned chocolate mousse cakes, caramel kisses, and raspberry tarts.

"All the gold you can see are layers of real gold, and all the cakes you see are delicious. I guarantee it."

He pointed at a large mirror and chest behind him. "And even though this looks like part of the wall, it is actually a secret door to the Queen's private apartments." Mr. O'Malley could barely contain his excitement. "And it is where Her Majesty will be entering to greet you today."

A murmuring of excited whispers filled the grand room.

"But first, there are a few rules you'll need to know about being in the presence of Her Majesty."

Holly wished she'd brought a notebook so she wouldn't forget a thing.

"When you greet the Queen, the correct formal address is 'Your Majesty,' and after that, you can simply say 'ma'am,' as in 'jam.' Men are to bow their heads while women do a small curtsy. You must never, under any circumstances, touch the Queen unless she offers you her hand, in which case you may shake it, but do not grip it tightly or pump it. Do not hug or kiss her, and whatever you do, do not ask about her famous grandchildren. She is very sensitive about that."

"I'm sure she's not as uptight as all that," Mrs. Trifle declared.

Holly could feel her chest tighten. "I think it's very important that we follow Mr. O'Malley's rules."

"After all," her mother said, as if Holly hadn't even spoken, "deep down, she's just like us, except for the castles and palaces and crowns."

"The Queen will be here in mere moments." Mr. O'Malley was doing his best to keep his emotions in check, even though it was obvious that he was jittery with excitement. "Are there any final questions before she arrives?"

"Can we take selfies?" Mr. Trifle was already thinking of how he could use the picture to promote the business.

"I'm afraid not. Her Majesty isn't one for selfies," Mr. O'Malley said.

"It's just an innocent photo," Mrs. Trifle argued. "I'm sure she'd love to."

"Her Majesty would rather you didn't."

"Oh, come on, O'Malley." Mr. Trifle put his arm around the Queen's representative's shoulders and squeezed them tighter than seemed comfortable. "What harm can it do?"

Mr. O'Malley recoiled as if a python had slithered around him, threatening to squeeze him to death. "It's not a matter of harm, but of—"

The wall behind Mr. O'Malley slowly opened, and out sprang two small yapping dogs followed by a small gray-haired lady wearing glasses, a pale yellow sweater set, and pearls.

"She's here." There was a gleam in Holly's eyes.

"It's really her." Mr. Kapoor's heart fluttered, and he worried he was in danger of passing out.

"Sorry I'm late," the Queen said. "I was hoping to be here when you arrived, but the corgis were having their baths, and it was a tad hard to convince them to get out."

Mr. O'Malley held out his hand. "Ladies and gentlemen, may I introduce you to the Head of the Commonwealth, Defender of the Faith, and official patron of the Most Marvelous International Spelling Bee, Her Majesty the Queen."

There was a rather awkward collection of bowing and curtsying and a quiet murmuring of "Your Majesty."

"Thank you, Mr. O'Malley. That is very kind."

Mr. O'Malley blushed from ear to ear.

"Welcome, everyone, to Buckingham Palace. My husband, the Prince, and I would like to congratulate you all on being part of this most marvelous competition. It takes hard work and intelligence to get here, but also great gumption. We wish you the very best of luck, and we look forward to settling back in our pajamas and watching you all on television. For now, please mingle and enjoy the delicious cakes. They are *scrumptious*."

Holly quickly flicked through her pages of notes to be

sure that she wouldn't forget a single rule Mr. O'Malley had told them.

The Trifles, on the other hand, seemed determined to break every one.

"Your Majesty." Mr. Trifle grabbed the Queen's hand and gave it a hearty shake. Her glasses slipped a little to the side. Palace security staff moved in to help, but she gave them a discreet nod that she was fine.

"My, what a strong grip you have!" She straightened her glasses.

"It's the muscles, you see. My wife, Mrs. Trifle, and I own our own fitness and beauty center."

Holly silently pleaded, *Please, please don't give her your—*

"Card?" Mr. Trifle whipped a card from his pocket. "It's called Beaut Butts and Guts. Guaranteed to get anyone's butt and gut in shape in no time."

He did it, Holly thought. *My dad actually said the word "butt" to the Queen of England. Twice!*

The entire room fell silent—except for the corgis, who growled.

Holly was sure they'd be kicked out or thrown in prison for their offenses.

The Queen, however, continued on with perfect grace and politely accepted the card. "You do look exceedingly fit."

"Thank you, ma'am." The Trifles smiled as if they had just

won the lottery, while Holly stood in a mire of mortification, and again, she wished she knew the address of her real parents—the ones who would never embarrass her like these ones. "We can show you some of our moves if you like."

Holly literally stopped breathing.

Mr. O'Malley tried to intervene. "Oh, that won't be—"

Before he could finish, Mr. and Mrs. Trifle tore off their outer clothes in one Velcro-ripping move, revealing shiny spandex suits underneath. Mr. Trifle began a series of jumping jacks and squats, while Mrs. Trifle lunged to each side. "These are two of our most effective moves to tone flab."

Mr. O'Malley turned white and looked as if he were about to pass out.

The royal guards exchanged puzzled looks, unsure if this was bizarre but harmless behavior or a serious security breach. No one had ever exercised in front of the Queen before.

"Do these every day, ma'am," Mr. Trifle said, "and you, too, can have butts like ours."

There was a very long pause. No one dared move.

Finally, the Queen said, "Congratulations to you"—she raised an eyebrow and gave a knowing smile—"and your well-toned butts and guts."

The Queen and her corgis moved to the table of cakes.

"How about that?" Mr. Trifle whispered. "She greatly admires our *butts.*"

"They *are* very fine," Mrs. Trifle agreed.

The Queen surveyed the selection of tasty morsels, deciding which one to pick, while the corgis sniffed at the cuffs of Boo's jeans. "Oh, they like you." She leaned in closer. "And trust me, they don't like everyone."

Mom tried to discreetly shuffle Boo by the shoulders so that he wasn't so close to the royal dogs.

"What's your name, young man?"

"Boo Wimple, and this is Mom, Dad, Nanna Flo, and my champion spelling sister, India."

"It is a pleasure to meet you all."

"Can I ask you a question?" Boo asked.

"Certainly."

"Do you like being Queen?"

"There is no greater pleasure or privilege. Even though I must admit that when it gets a bit chaotic, I sneak through the secret door to my room and read. When I come back, I often find no one has even noticed I'm gone."

"Is it hard being surrounded by people all the time, watching everything you do?" Boo asked.

The Queen had a wistful look. "It isn't all the time. They do let me sleep in peace, but it would be nice to walk down the street or through a park completely unrecognized. I do love being Queen, but if I could have one afternoon of just being anonymous, I think that would be rather nice."

"You could come to Yungabilla and be incognito," Boo suggested.

She chuckled. "And where's that?"

"It's in Australia. It's super quiet, and everyone's really nice. Except Bessie, but that's only when there are lamingtons around."

"Bessie?"

"Farmer Austin's cow."

"I see. I may have to visit one day." The Queen turned to India. "And how about you, India? Are you ready for your big day?"

"I think so, ma'am. I am a little bit nervous."

"It's only natural," the Queen said. "There have been times when I've been terribly nervous, especially when I first became Queen. I used to have this voice in my head that was very negative."

"Me too!" India remembered the voice in her head during the first spelling bee. "But it went away."

"I suspect it's because you held up your chin and got on with it. As my good friend the former prime minister used to say, 'Attitude is a little thing that makes a big difference.'"

"Were you always a good speller?" India was curious.

"My sister and I would lie in bed at night and have

competitions. Papa would often come into our rooms and sternly tell us to turn out the lights. He could be very strict, you know, being King and all. We would dutifully say good night, but when he was gone, we'd take out our flashlights and keep playing, and we wouldn't go to sleep until one of us was the champion."

"Who usually won?"

"I don't like to boast, but I was quite good." The Queen chuckled and chose a bite-size chocolate mousse cake. "I better mingle. I wish all the spellers well, of course, but I will especially look forward to watching you."

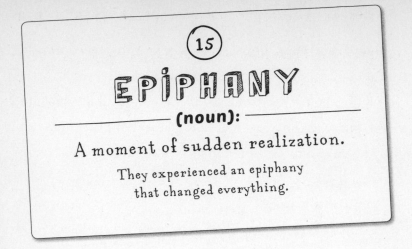

15

EPIPHANY

(noun):

A moment of sudden realization.

They experienced an epiphany
that changed everything.

"INGENIOUS INDIA HAD NEVER BEEN in a situation that was so *perilous*."

That afternoon, in preparation for round one of the Most Marvelous International Spelling Bee, Mom told another story of *Brave Boo and Ingenious India* for some last-minute practice. This time, she'd written it down so Boo could double-check the spelling.

"Perilous," India said. "P-e-r-i-l-o-u-s."

Boo held Mom's story in his hands, nodding at every word.

"She was dangling from a helicopter high above Buckingham Palace, which was *ablaze*."

"A-b-l-a-z-e."

"Fire consumed the building, and now the only way out was

up. The pilot, Brave Boo, held the chopper steady against the waves of rising heat, while India *descended…*"

"D-e-s-c-e-n-d-e-d."

"…into a moment that was truly *valiant…*"

"V-a-l-i-a-n-t."

"…and rescued the Queen from certain *catastrophe.*"

"C-a-t-a-s-t-r-o-p-h-e."

"A perfect score!" Boo cried.

"Just as I expected." Dad had been tense up until now. He sat back in the armchair as if he knew all along how well it would go.

"Someone tell the other spellers not to bother turning up," Nanna Flo decided. "India Wimple is here."

Normally, Mom frowned at this kind of talk. She didn't want to build India's hopes up only to have them dashed. She also wanted to remind everyone that winning wasn't what competing was all about.

But today, even she joined in.

"You're going to be magnificent!" She kissed her daughter on the forehead.

The India of Mom's stories was brave and adventurous, and Boo was daring and invincible. India always knew how to get out of scrapes, and Boo could scale tall buildings and face the meanest of bad guys.

India always thought Mom told the stories so they could feel like heroes, but she wondered now if that's how Mom saw her kids—stronger and more courageous than they actually were.

"Wimple family," Mom announced. "Get dressed! Let's deliver this champion to her destiny!"

~~~~~

Not far away in another suite at the Royal Windsor Hotel, Grandpop Eriksson poked his head into his grandson's bedroom. "Can I come in?"

Grandpop was wearing a suit that was a little too big and had combed what little hair he had into a neat swirl.

"Sure." Peter was sitting in bed with his dictionary nestled on his lap.

"I'm nervous," Peter said.

"It's to be expected. It's a nervous kind of day." Grandpop Eriksson sat on the edge of the bed and handed him a small locket. "Do you recognize this?"

"That's Grandma's."

"Open it."

Inside was a tiny photo of Peter as a baby surrounded by his mom, Grandpop, and Grandma.

"We were so happy when you came along. It was one of the best days of my life. Your grandma would be so proud of you. I am too, even though I haven't been very good at showing it. Since she died, I haven't quite been myself and have disappeared a little."

"You've been sad."

"We all were. I never knew you could miss someone so much, but that's no excuse. I should have been there for you with school, especially with your dad not being here."

Peter felt a jab in his chest. He'd never spoken about his dad with Grandpop. After his dad had left, Grandma would take him for walks, cuddle him at night, and tell him to let it out if he was angry or upset, but with Mom and Grandpop, it never seemed right.

"Your grandma would be really cross with me for not stepping up. From now on, I promise, you can count on me."

"Thanks, Grandpop." Peter held out the locket.

"You keep it close, to remind you that we're all on your side. Now, let's go show those others how to spell."

~~~~~~

Down the hall, the Trifles were making their own preparations for the bee.

"Sit still." Mrs. Trifle twirled another lock of hair around the curling iron. Holly felt as if her head were on fire.

"I'd prefer to read, if that's OK."

"How is reading going to help you get ready for your big night?" Mrs. Trifle tugged at another lock. "When you walk into a room, people won't be judging you on how many books you've read. When I'm finished, they'll be amazed by how pretty you look."

"I'd rather read than look pretty."

Her mother scowled. "There's a good chance of that happening, but we can at least try. Now sit still and let me work my magic."

Mrs. Trifle continued to pull and yank at Holly's hair.

"I know you think your father and I work too hard, but it's for the family, which is, after all, the most important thing in life."

"It's what happens when you have kids." Mr. Trifle huffed as he lifted dumbbells. "You want to do everything for them. It's only natural."

"But this reading business is going to get you nowhere." Mrs. Trifle took a brush and began fluffing out the curls. "Your father and I never bothered with books, and look at us! We're the epiphany of success!"

Holly knew her mother meant the *epitome* of success, as in the perfect example of success, but she didn't want to upset her, so she said nothing.

"There." Mrs. Trifle stood back and admired Holly's hair, which ballooned around her head like she'd stuck a finger in an electrical socket. "You should be right on time." She flopped onto the couch with a heavy sigh. "I could sleep for a week."

"Aren't you coming?" Holly asked.

"Not now, Molly." She placed two slices of cucumber over her eyes. "I need to rest. It's been a very big day."

Mr. Trifle saw Holly's shoulders slump, and something in that small gesture made his heart jolt. At first, he worried it was the beginning of a heart attack, but that was all it was: a small, melancholy jolt.

"I'll go with you," he found himself saying.

"You will?" Holly had to make sure she hadn't misheard or that her father wasn't talking to someone else.

Mr. Trifle thought about it. "Sure. That way, your mom can have some peace and quiet."

Mr. Trifle put on a fresh shirt, and Holly raced to her room for her sweater. She was about to say goodbye to her mom when she heard the faint ripples of snoring and realized she'd already fallen asleep.

"Come on," Mr. Trifle said. "We better not be late."

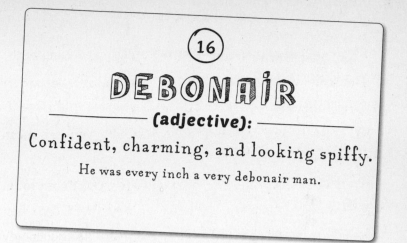

16

DEBONAIR

(adjective):

Confident, charming, and looking spiffy.

He was every inch a very debonair man.

"THE DAY WE'VE ALL BEEN waiting for has finally arrived."

Mr. O'Malley beamed at the bustling crowd from the stage of the Heritage Ballroom of the Royal Windsor Hotel. He was immaculately dressed in a royal-blue pinstripe suit with a bright-red cravat and flower in his lapel that were almost the same color as his cheeks.

"Round one of the Most Marvelous International Spelling Bee will begin shortly, so please take your seats."

The ballroom buzzed with contestants, parents, and a television crew setting up cameras and lights.

India looked up at the stage. Rows of seats were arranged for the spellers on one side, a podium for the pronouncer on the other, and in the center was a single microphone where *millions* of people would soon watch her spell. Her stomach twisted into an entire basket of knots. The Wimples huddled together with their red scarves tucked around their necks.

India tugged at her purple dress with yellow sunflowers, a hand-me-down from Mrs. Rahim's eldest daughter. "Do you think I'll be OK?"

"Of course you will," Dad said. "You're a Wimple. You'll be amazing."

"It's true!" Nanna Flo said. "Or you can dunk me in barbecue sauce and serve me for dinner."

"But what if I freeze onstage?" India fiddled with the contestant's number dangling from her neck. "Like I did before? You know, when…"

She couldn't bring herself to say it, but what she meant was this: what if she froze like she did during her school play, *Matilda*, when she saw her mom and dad in the back of the auditorium, carrying Boo outside while he was having a serious asthma attack? She was left onstage, stumbling through her lines, which she mostly forgot, wondering the whole time if her brother was going to be OK.

"That was a long time ago," Dad said. "And since then, you've become Australia's spelling champion." He put his hand on his heart and stuck his nose into the air. "And my personal hero."

Boo copied his dad. "And mine too."

Nanna Flo and Mom followed. "Us too."

India laughed. "OK, you can stop now. People are starting to stare." But she did feel better.

"Have you got your lucky hanky?" Nanna Flo asked.

"Yes." India tapped the pocket where she kept the hanky Nanna had given her for the first spelling bee.

"Good luck hug?" Boo held out his arms.

"Yes, please."

"You'll be great, Sis," he declared. "I know it."

Mom kissed her on each cheek. "Take a long, steadying breath before each word, and try to have fun."

Dad gave her one of his special hugs, which felt like being wrapped in a warm, fuzzy blanket. "We'll be cheering for you."

It was then that India noticed Nanna searching the room. "Looking for anyone special?"

"No." Nanna Flo clutched her purse. "Why would I be looking for anyone special? I was admiring the ballroom. Can't a woman admire a ballroom?"

India frowned. Nanna Flo was rambling, which was something she never did.

India reached up and placed her hand on Nanna's forehead. "You don't seem to have a temperature."

"Of course I don't. I feel perfectly fine."

That was when Mr. Eriksson and Peter wound their way through the crowd. "Florence." He smiled. "Stood up to any bullies since I last saw you?"

"No, I've been busy," Nanna Flo said. "Rescued anyone from any falling banners?"

"Nah, I'm leaving that to the young ones."

Nanna Flo giggled. *Again.*

So did Mr. Eriksson.

The Wimples were confused.

"Would you mind if I sat with you?" Mr. Eriksson asked.

"Can't see why not." Nanna held up her bulging purse, "I've brought enough treats for everyone."

"Good luck, kids." Grandpop Eriksson followed Nanna Flo and the Wimples into the audience.

"He's happier than he's been in a while," Peter said. "He spent half an hour in front of the mirror deciding how to do his hair, and he doesn't have that much."

"Nanna Flo's been acting weird too." India watched as they made their way to their seats. "I've never heard her giggle until this trip, and now she can't seem to stop."

On cue, they heard her giggle once more.

"All right, spellers." Esmerelda's voice cut through the crowd. "If you're not onstage in the next three minutes, you're out."

"I guess we better go." India tried to pep herself up. "Ready?"

Peter nodded. "I think so."

Something about his expression made India think about being caught in a storm. She knew that feeling from the first spelling bee—swamped and totally overwhelmed.

"We're going to be fine." She stuck her chin in the air, surprised that she actually meant it.

"Even if I fall on my face?"

"You won't fall on your face," India said. "But we'll pick you up if you do."

Peter gave her a weak smile. "Thank you."

"All part of the service."

They climbed onto the stage, which was filling with the last of the spellers. Rajish, Summer, and Holly waved them over.

"We saved you seats," Rajish said before turning to India. "I know there's no hope of winning while you're here, but I thought I'd come anyway."

"It was nice of you to make the effort."

"Will you let me hold the trophy when it's yours?"

India laughed. "I'll think about it."

Holly fiddled with the ends of her braids. "I'm so nervous, I have to remind myself to keep breathing."

"I'm so nervous, I forgot my name when Esmerelda asked."

Peter clasped his hands so tightly that his knuckles turned white. "Grandpop had to say it for me."

"I'm not nervous at all," Summer announced, as if this were any old regular day and *not* an internationally televised competition.

"Really?" Peter gazed in admiration. "Not even a little?"

"Maybe a little," Summer admitted.

"So you're human after all?" Rajish asked.

"Yes," Summer said as she brushed down her skirt, "but a very stylish one."

"Ladies, gentlemen, and spellers," Mr. O'Malley enthused from the podium. The audience settled into an anxious hush. "We're only moments away from one of the most exciting events of your lives."

India saw Esmerelda yawn from the wings of the stage.

"To get us underway, it is time to meet your spelling bee pronouncer." There was an audible gasp in the room. "It is my tremendous pleasure to introduce the magnificent Fozdrake Magnifico."

A flood of cheers filled the ballroom as the pencil-thin, debonair man in a bright-yellow suit and pointy winklepicker shoes bounded onto the stage. His sleek, black hair was swept into a perfect wave above a glimmering, movie-star smile.

"It's Fozdrake!" Holly's hands flew to her mouth, worried that she might actually scream.

"Is it really him?" Peter's fears faded a little at the sight of the world-famous pronouncer.

"It is." Even Summer was excited. "The one and only."

Fozdrake blew a kiss to the audience, who went wild.

Mr. O'Malley stood in the wings, equally awed by Fozdrake's appearance. He stood beside Esmerelda, who, it was safe to say, was not so charmed.

Fozdrake had been bathed in cheers for most of his life. As a child, he had performed on a television show called *Future Stars*.

He was a dancer and was often compared to his hero, a man called Fred Astaire, who was so light on his feet that Fozdrake was sure his shoes were filled with helium.

Fozdrake was *Future Stars'* main star. The dancers appeared at shopping centers, onstage, and even embarked on a world tour.

Then, on the day of Fozdrake's sixteenth birthday, he was dropped from the show. That was part of the contract—you stayed until you turned sixteen, then you were on your own.

After that, he appeared on home shopping channels and on *Dancing Under the Stars* with other forgotten childhood Future Stars, but it wasn't until he became pronouncer of the Most Marvelous International Spelling Bee that he rediscovered some of his former fame and glory.

"Spellers, *are…you…ready*?" He threw his arms into the air.

"Yes…we…are!" The children cried out in unison.

"Good luck," Rajish whispered to India.

"You too," India whispered back.

"As you know," Fozdrake continued, "the Most Marvelous International Spelling Bee will be screened all over the world. In a matter of moments, the lights will lower, and the broadcast will begin. I will summon each speller to the microphone, where millions of admiring fans will marvel at your magnificence. So banish those butterflies, dispel those doubts, and—"

A great crackling hiss sounded from above, and a shower of sparks rained onto the stage, followed by a large metal lighting box.

Fozdrake screeched and scurried out of the way, only just avoiding the box as it clattered to the stage. Twisted metal and broken glass fanned across the polished floor.

The lights flashed, and the ballroom was plunged into darkness.

After a few moments, Mr. O'Malley's face could be seen onstage, illuminated by the light of his phone. "Please stay calm, everyone. We will solve this problem in no time."

"What's going on?" Holly asked.

"The falling light might have caused a blackout." India saw the silhouettes of stagehands comforting Fozdrake and leading him into the wings.

Hotel staff with flashlights flittered into the room like fireflies, while Esmerelda gave directions to the workers. Maintenance people checked the fuse boxes and wiring and spoke in hushed tones to Mr. O'Malley. He took a hanky from his pocket and wiped his brow. He'd been doing his best to appear cheery, but as he turned away, India saw that he looked utterly downhearted.

"Do you think the spelling bee will still go on?" Peter seemed stuck in that storm again.

"Of course it will," India said. "Mr. O'Malley will make sure of it."

"But we haven't been very lucky so far," Holly said. "First the falling banner in the lobby, then the escaped animals during dinner, and now this."

"It's true." Rajish thought about it. "It's as if someone doesn't want the spelling bee to happen."

"Why would anyone want to stop the bee?" India asked.

"Maybe they're jealous of how very clever we are," Summer decided.

"Or how *humble* we are?" Rajish suggested.

"Yes, that too." Summer smiled.

Prince Harry poked his head out of Peter's pocket. "Are you nervous too, little fella?" When Peter scooped him out, a photo fell from his pocket. It was bent, ragged around the edges, and showed a man holding a baby.

India handed it back. "Is that you and your dad?"

Peter nodded. "I'm a little taller now," he joked. "I know this will sound silly, but I'm hoping that if he's watching, he might recognize me and see that I turned out OK."

Prince Harry tickled Peter's cheek with his soft spines.

"You turned out more than *OK*," India said.

"You're funny and smart," Holly said.

"And a champion speller," Rajish added.

They all looked to Summer. India raised her eyebrows, making it clear it was her turn to say something nice.

"And…you're…kind to lizards."

"And that's just *four* of your special qualities," India said. "Wait until he finds out all the others."

Prince Harry jumped from his hand to his shoulder, where he nuzzled Peter's neck.

Holly smiled. "And Prince Harry agrees."

Peter felt his bottom lip quiver and a lump form in his throat. He hadn't been called a namby-pamby in days, and the last of Bruiser's bruises had almost disappeared. Apart from his family, he'd rarely been complimented in his life.

Before he could say anything, Mr. O'Malley's face was lit by a flashlight, hollowing out his cheeks and eye sockets and giving him a strange, haunted look.

"Could I have your attention?" Even though he was trying to be cheerful, India knew from the tremble in his voice that he didn't have good news. "I'm afraid there's been a major power surge that will take some time to fix, so it is with a heavy heart that I announce tonight's first round of the Most Marvelous International Spelling Bee is…postponed."

Sighs of disappointment rose into the air like a thick fog. As well as a few disgruntled complaints.

Mr. O'Malley deflated like an old party balloon until he lifted himself higher and tried to sound more upbeat. "You have my solemn promise that this is merely a temporary setback. We will have the power restored and everything in readiness for one of the most marvelous days of your lives."

As everyone in the room gathered their things and began to leave, India couldn't stop thinking about what Rajish had said. The idea that someone would deliberately sabotage the spelling bee was ridiculous. Wasn't it? Why would someone want to ruin a competition for kids, one that was loved around the world and by the Queen of England herself?

It didn't make any sense.

But no matter how much she tried to convince herself it couldn't be true, her suspicions just wouldn't budge.

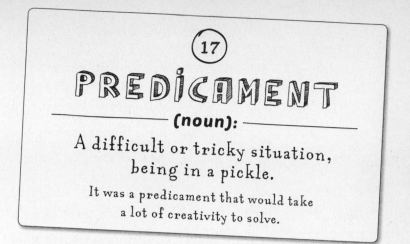

17

PREDICAMENT

(noun):

A difficult or tricky situation,
being in a pickle.

It was a predicament that would take
a lot of creativity to solve.

THE WIMPLES SAT ON THE couch in their hotel suite, and as Nanna Flo stood before them in an apricot dress and matching jacket that she only wore on special occasions, she held up different scarves, wondering which one worked better.

"What about this one?"

"That looks very elegant," Dad said, positive that Nanna Flo had shown them that one already.

She chose another. "Or maybe this one?"

"That's my favorite." Boo was sure they'd also seen this one already.

"I could always go with Daryl's red scarf to match the belt."

"That's good too." India had never heard Nanna talk so much about clothing.

Nanna Flo still couldn't choose. "Maybe it's the dress that's all wrong."

The Wimples secretly sighed. They'd spent an hour watching Nanna Flo parade all the dresses she'd brought to London before finally deciding on this one. They couldn't go through it again.

"I like that dress the best." India tried to sound resolute, even though she thought Nanna Flo looked perfect in whatever dress she wore.

"Me too!" Boo added. "It brings out your natural charm."

Boo had never said this to anyone before—he'd only ever heard it in movies—and was really hoping it would do the trick.

It didn't.

Nanna Flo flopped beside them on the couch. "Maybe this is a bad idea. I should stay here instead. Yes, that's it," she decided. "I'll stay and help India practice."

"There's no need," India said. "I have Mom, Dad, and Boo."

Mom picked up the blue scarf and gently draped it around Nanna Flo's neck. "I think this one suits you best."

Boo picked up her purse. "And you'll need this for any treats you sneak home for us."

Nanna Flo still didn't look sure until Dad kissed her on the cheek. "All you need to do now is have fun."

The Wimples stood in front of Nanna Flo.

"And tell us all about it when you get back," India added.

"But I—"

The doorbell rang. No one moved, including Nanna Flo, who looked up as if she'd heard a huge explosion.

"I'll get it." Boo jumped up from the couch and opened the door to find Mr. Eriksson. He was wearing a very fine suit and holding a bunch of flowers.

"Mr. Eriksson," Boo said. "Come in. Nanna's waiting for you."

"Good evening, Wimples." He handed the flowers to Nanna Flo. "Lovely to see you again, Florence."

Nanna Flo held the flowers and said nothing.

"She thinks it's lovely to see you too." India looked at her grandmother pointedly. "Don't you, Nanna?"

She nodded, still not saying a word.

This was going to be trickier than the Wimples thought—Nanna Flo was rarely at a loss for words.

Dad broke through the awkward silence. "Where are you off to?"

"I've booked a horse-drawn carriage ride around Hyde Park, followed by dinner at a karaoke restaurant."

"Karaoke?" Nanna Flo finally spoke up.

Mr. Eriksson shared a sneaky smile with the Wimples. "A

little bird told me you are quite the singer and once even sang at the Sydney Opera House."

"It was just one time and—"

"She was magnificent," Boo said.

India nodded. "Some say it was the best performance the Opera House has ever seen."

"Oh stop." Nanna Flo waved a hand.

"As your family, we have the right to boast," Dad said.

"It's part of the deal of being a Wimple." Mom kissed Nanna Flo on the cheek.

Mr. Eriksson held out his arm. "Shall we?"

The Wimples stood together in that huddling penguin way and smiled, which seemed to make Nanna finally relax. "Yes, we shall."

~~~~~

That night, the Wimples ordered Chinese takeout and held a mock spelling bee, which left India's head swimming with words. Boo was the pronouncer, and Mom and Dad were the adoring crowd. They cheered and whooped, and at times, Dad even burst into song, which, luckily for the Wimples and their neighbors, didn't last long.

As Boo and Mom dragged themselves to bed, India and Dad sat in the glow of her bedside light and practiced with her favorite dictionary, a present from the prime minister.

Dad opened the book and searched each page for the trickiest words he could find.

Antidisestablishmentarianism.

India spelled it perfectly.

Bibliothecarial.

This was harder, so India took her time, imagining each of the letters before she began.

Eudaemonia.

India folded her arms and gave her dad a skeptical look. "You've made that up."

"No, I haven't. It means a contented state of being happy, healthy, and prosperous, which perfectly describes me."

"You're not that prosperous."

"Ahhh, but you see, that's where you're wrong. I'm as rich a man as ever lived."

"Have you had a chance to talk to Mom about Boo?" India asked.

"I thought it'd be easier to tackle world peace first, then move on to Boo."

"He needs us, Dad."

"I know. I'll figure something out."

They heard the door of their suite open. It was Nanna Flo. And she was humming.

She poked her head in India's room. "Can I join in?"

Dad patted the bed. "How was it?"

Nanna Flo put down her purse and made herself comfortable. "Fun. He's not a very good singer, but don't tell him I told you. How are things here?"

"We need your help with a tricky predicament," India said.

"Anything."

"It's about Boo."

"Boo! Is he all right? Did he have another attack? I knew I shouldn't have gone out."

"He's *fine*, but he wants us to stop worrying about him— like now."

"We care about him."

"I know," India said, "but he's tired of being treated like a little kid."

"I guess he is getting older."

"And he wants to go back to school."

"Holy cow's udder, that's serious."

"That's not all." Dad's worry wrinkle was back. "He wants a dog."

"It might be easier to get him to the moon."

"That's what I said."

"Please, Nanna," India pleaded. "Boo needs our help."

She nodded. "And he'll have it. I might need a good strong cup of tea before I do it, but count me in."

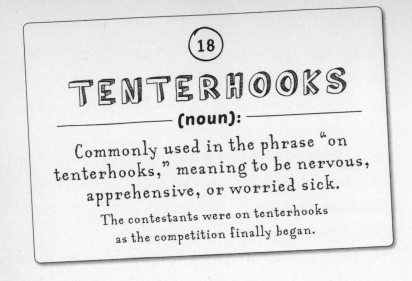

TENTERHOOKS

(noun):

Commonly used in the phrase "on tenterhooks," meaning to be nervous, apprehensive, or worried sick.

The contestants were on tenterhooks as the competition finally began.

"WELCOME TO THE FIFTIETH ANNIVERSARY of the Most Marvelous International Spelling Bee!"

It was the next day, and Fozdrake had spruced himself up for the second attempt at round one. The theme music played, the cameras rolled, and a single spotlight glimmered off the silver sequined letters sewn into his blue suit.

He waited for the applause to fade.

"And welcome to our wonderful viewers watching from around the world. Over two evenings, you will behold a battle of bravery from superlative spellers. It will be demanding, it will be draining, but most of all, it will reveal our supreme spelling superstar."

Fozdrake basked in the applause, teeth twinkling, eyes sparkling.

"And now, it is time to welcome our spelling supremos." He flung out his hand, and the stage lights snapped on, revealing rows of apprehensive children seated onstage.

When the clapping died down, Fozdrake continued. "This is a knockout competition, which means when the word is spelled incorrectly, the contestant, sadly, must leave the stage." He leaned toward the camera, and his voice grew serious. "By the end of tonight, only half of our wondrous wordsmiths will remain."

India felt as if a rock had fallen on her stomach. She worried that she might be sick, until Rajish flashed her a comforting smile.

Holly pulled at the tip of her braid, and Peter was the color of a bedsheet. Summer's gleaming smile, of course, never faltered. Not once.

"The valorous victor will receive a check for the tantalizing total of "—Fozdrake raised an eyebrow—"ten thousand dollars." The audience *oohed*. "And that's not all. They will be the proud proprietor of this!"

With a deft flick of his hand, Fozdrake removed a dark cloth from a stand beside him. Beneath it was the Most Marvelous International Spelling Bee trophy.

The audience gasped.

Perched on a glass stand, it seemed to float above the stage.

The lights gave it a golden glow that made it look more like one of the crown jewels than a mere trophy.

"There it is." Peter gazed at the polished cup, which rose from the pages of an open brass book.

"It's beautiful." India thought it looked even more impressive in real life than on their TV in Yungabilla.

"It's so much bigger than I imagined," Holly marveled.

"But who will possess this prestigious prize?" Fozdrake turned to the spellers, his eyes wide and searching. "Which one of you will walk away the winner?"

Peter sat on his hands to stop them from shaking. He knew the person who won that trophy would be in all the magazines, splashed up on millions of TVs and across the internet.

His dad would *have* to see him then.

Prince Harry wriggled inside his jacket. Peter glanced down to see his shiny nose poking out. "Thanks, Prince Harry."

"Spellers." Fozdrake's melodious voice reverberated throughout the hall. "*Are…you…ready?*"

"Yes…we…are!" The children cried out in unison.

"Then let the Most Marvelous International Spelling Bee…begin!"

Music played, and spotlights beamed over the crowd as Fozdrake plucked the official word cards from his pocket.

India spotted Mr. O'Malley in the wings, nervously pacing and brushing invisible fluff from his jacket. Esmerelda stood beside him, holding her clipboard. She wore a stony expression and seemed thoroughly unperturbed, if not a little bored.

"I call the first contestant: Freya Rose."

A girl with a mop of bouncy orange curls almost ran to the microphone.

"Are you ready, Freya?"

She pushed a bunch of curls behind her ears, but they immediately escaped. "Yes, Mr. Magnifico."

"Your first word is *effervescent*," Fozdrake read with perfect pronunciation. "This is an adjective meaning energetic or bubbly."

Freya didn't hesitate. "E-f-f-e-r-v-e-s-c-e-n-t. Effervescent."

"That is correct!"

Mr. O'Malley and the crowd breathed out in a collective sigh of relief and applauded as Freya and her curls bounced back to her seat.

"Our next contestant is Barnaby Gray."

Fozdrake craned his head, searching through the rows of children, but no one moved.

"Barnaby? Are you here?"

There was a long pause before a boy raised his head, a deep frown wrinkling his brow. He rose unsteadily to his feet and shuffled across the stage like he were carrying a heavy sack. He played with his tie, which dangled from a tightly buttoned collar.

"Barnaby, your word is *lugubrious*—an adjective meaning glum, gloomy, or down in the dumps."

The boy stared at the ground for so long that Fozdrake wondered if he should repeat the word.

"Lugubrious," the boy began. "L-u-g-u-…"

He tugged at his collar, finding it hard to breathe.

"…b-r-i-u-s. Lugubrious."

"Oh dear," Fozdrake said. "I'm sorry, but that is…incorrect."

The boy nodded. Then began to cry.

"But what an excellent effort to have made it this far," Fozdrake said, trying to lift his mood.

Barnaby quietly whimpered and dragged his feet as he trudged off the stage.

Ever the professional, Fozdrake snapped back to his chirpier self. More contestants were called, and more words were spelled.

Exertion.

Assiduous.

Industrious.

Some did a little dance when they were correct, while others stormed off or were coaxed from the stage by embarrassed parents.

The number of spellers dwindled.

"Our next speller is Holly Trifle."

Holly gripped the seat so hard that Peter thought she might not get up.

"You have to leave the chair here," he whispered, "or Esmerelda will be furious."

Holly released her grip but still didn't get up.

"Go get 'em, Holly Trifle," Peter said.

She stood slowly and focused on every footstep so she didn't trip on her way to the microphone.

"Holly, your word is *tenterhooks*. This is a noun meaning hooks used to fix cloth to a drying frame. The phrase 'on tenter-hooks' means to be apprehensive or nervous."

"Tenterhooks." Holly tugged at the end of her braid. She could see the letters laid out in her mind. All she had to do was spell it, just as she saw it. "T-e-n-t…"

But then she faltered. She knew *e* came next, but what if she was wrong? What if it was an *a* or an *o*? She felt her whole body heat up in a rush of dread.

"You have fifteen seconds left, Holly." Even Fozdrake was on tenterhooks, no matter how you spelled it.

Not a sound could be heard in the auditorium—until Holly heard her mother's voice in her head: *This time, don't blow it.*

The voice entered like a bad wind, blowing the word away so

that her mind went blank. As hard as Holly tried, she couldn't see any letters at all.

Her mouth went dry, and her throat pinched.

Holly knew it was all over. She was going to fail on the first word; she was going to blow it after all.

She lowered her head and turned to leave but was stopped by Summer, India, Rajish, and Peter, who were staring straight at her. Peter held up double crossed fingers. Rajish and India clasped their hands while Summer gave her a confident nod.

The word reappeared in Holly's mind.

And it was right. She was sure of it.

She spun back to the microphone before her time ran out. "...e-r-h-o-o-k-s. Tenterhooks."

Fozdrake's face was a picture of composure. It was impossible to tell what he was thinking. Holly tried to read his thoughts, until finally, he cried, "That is correct!"

The audience erupted in applause.

Holly jumped on the spot and pounded a fist in the air. Her friends gave her a thumbs-up in support as she rushed back to her seat.

"I knew you could do it," Peter said as she sat beside him. Prince Harry stuck his head out of Peter's pocket and poked his tongue at Holly, making her laugh. "Harry knew it too."

The competition was now in full swing. The tension sizzled in the air. Mr. O'Malley pulled out his hanky more than once to wipe his brow. Esmerelda yawned.

Conviction.

Fortitude.

Determination.

"The next speller is Summer Millicent Ernestine Beauregard-Champion."

Summer strode to the microphone, oozing confidence, and waved at the audience. "I'm ready, Mr. Magnifico."

"Your word is *imperturbable*. This is an adjective meaning composed, collected, or cool as a cucumber."

Summer raised her jaw and clasped her hands in front of her, as if she were about to launch into song. "I-m-p-e-r-t-u-r-b-a-b-l-e. Imperturbable."

"That is correct!"

Fozdrake called more names, and as each word was misspelled, another child departed the stage, leaving more and more empty chairs.

"I would like to call to the microphone India Wimple."

From the back of the auditorium, India heard a cheer and knew it was Nanna Flo. She gave a discreet wave and walked to the microphone.

"You have a fan?" Fozdrake asked.

"My nanna." India nodded. "She gets a little excited."

The audience chuckled.

"Your word is *devotee*, a noun meaning an enthusiastic fan or admirer."

There are moments in every speller's bee when they hear their next word and are filled with either fear or relief. For India, this was a moment of wonderful relief.

"D-e-v-o-t-e-e. Devotee."

"Which you are lucky to have," Fozdrake said. "And spell correctly."

Nanna Flo let out another cheer. Esmerelda Stomp poked her head out from behind the curtain and scowled into the audience. It seems cheering was something else she'd liked banned from the bee.

"I now call Peter Eriksson."

A bolt of panic gripped Peter. This was it. This was his chance to make his dad proud. He did his best to look confident and took his position at the microphone. As he smiled for the cameras—and secretly for his dad—he silently begged, *Please, please get this right.*

"Peter, your word is…*triskaidekaphobia*. This is the—"

"Fear of the number thirteen," Peter blurted. "It's one of my favorite words. It has been since I was little. I've always thought it's odd to have a word for something so specific, don't you think?"

Esmerelda glared at the garrulous boy.

"I agree." Fozdrake smiled. "Now let's hear you spell it."

Peter took a calming breath and began. "T-r-i-s-k-a-i-d-e-k-a-p-h-o-b-i-a. Triskaidekaphobia."

"And that, Peter Eriksson, is correct!"

The audience applauded. Peter waved at the camera, hoping his dad knew he was waving at him.

Rajish was next with *charisma*, while Holly hesitantly spelled *pusillanimous*. Summer breezed through *insouciance*, and India took her time with *elucubrate*. When Peter was asked to spell *forefather*, he took it as a sign that his father must be watching.

After only a few more spellers, Fozdrake announced, "With the next misspelled word, we will have our grand finalists."

He let the possibility of those words hang in the air. Each remaining speller knew they were one step away from the grand final but only one incorrect letter away from leaving.

"Millie Olsen, it's your turn."

It was the girl India had seen in the lobby with the yellow ribbons and overzealous mother.

"Your word is *harangue*. This can be a noun or a verb, meaning criticism or to be lectured or berated."

The girl was shaking so much, her dress quivered. "Harangue." She looked into the audience, as if searching for an answer.

Come on, India thought. *You can do this.*

"Fifteen seconds, Millie," Fozdrake tried to say as gently as he could.

"H-a-r-a…" She wrote the word on her hand. "…n…g…" She shook her head and started over in her mind. "…e?"

Fozdrake took longer than usual to reply. "Millie, I'm afraid that is…incorrect."

Millie nodded and almost immediately stopped shaking.

The pronouncer looked at the crestfallen girl. "Millie Olsen, let me congratulate you for your courage and praise you for your poise. You are spectacular for having succeeded this far into the competition. Don't we agree, audience?"

The crowd rose to their feet, applauding and cheering Millie, who attempted a brave smile, when a woman ran down the center aisle, waving her arms and screaming. "Nooooo!"

A furious look planted itself on Esmerelda's face.

"She deserves a second chance!"

Esmerelda was not having it. She jabbed her finger at two security guards, who hurried toward the distraught woman, trying to intercept her before she reached the stage.

"All those tutoring fees!" the woman cried, crumbling to the floor, sobbing. "Wasted! I'll sue! Mark my words!"

The guards struggled to help her to her feet; her body was weighed down by disappointment. They gently redirected her to the exit, followed by the diminished figure of Millie. Her voice faded as the door closed behind her.

Fozdrake carried on with unflappable ease. "Ladies and gentlemen, I give you the Most Marvelous International Spelling Bee Grand Finalists!"

The audience sprang from their chairs again. There was no stopping them. Mr. O'Malley lost himself momentarily and threw his arms around Esmerelda, who couldn't decide what made her more furious—the unruly audience or the uncalled-for hug.

"We did it?" Holly wanted to make sure.

"Of course we did," Summer said through closed teeth, making sure to beam at the cameras before they stopped filming.

Rajish leaned over to India. "Nice work."

"You too." India felt so happy, she thought she might float out of her chair.

Fozdrake let the cheers whirl around him as he made his final farewell. "Tune in tomorrow for the grand final, when we discover who among these finalists will be the spelling champion of the world! I'm Fozdrake Magnifico, and until then, may your evening be most marvelous."

He blew the audience a kiss, which sent them into a frenzy.

When the broadcast was over and the music had ended, Mr. and Mrs. Kapoor were the first parents onstage, smothering Rajish in hugs and kisses.

"My son!" Mr. Kapoor was crying. "My beautiful, clever son!"

The Wimples raced up the steps, with Dad equally teary.

Mr. Eriksson swept his grandson off his feet. "I knew you could do it, Peter! I just *knew* it!"

"I made it through!" Summer was on the phone with her parents. "I'm in the grand final!"

Holly watched all the hugging and crying, and her heart ached just a little. She was used to seeing other parents make a fuss over their kids—at debate tournaments, school plays, or sports contests. It always happened. It's not that she didn't enjoy other people's happiness, but these were the times when she thought about her real parents. The ones who would have swung her into the air and cheered like mad about how proud they were.

"You were really good."

Holly turned to the voice behind her. It was her dad, who seemed a trifle shocked. "And under so much pressure." He shook his head in wonderment. "My daughter. A champion speller."

And in that moment, Holly saw something in her father's eyes that she had never seen before. It looked like pride. And it was because of her.

"You really could win this," he said, as if he only just now realized.

Making it through the first round made Holly feel dizzy, but hearing her dad call her a champion made her feel as if she were flying.

"Can I have your attention?" Mr. O'Malley stood beside Fozdrake, positively ebullient with how smoothly the first round of the bee had run. His face was a beacon of admiration for the spellers before him. "Congratulations to all of you and to Mr. Magnifico for his usual perfect pronunciation! We look forward to more moments of brilliance during the grand final when—"

Mr. O'Malley said no more, because a *whooping* alarm bellowed throughout the ballroom.

"Fire!" a voice wailed.

Fear quickly spread, and people rushed from the room.

Mr. O'Malley watched on, rigid with fright, until Esmerelda shoved him out of the way and snatched the microphone. "Head to your closest exit and make your way to the assembly point outside the hotel," she barked.

Parents scrambled to reach their kids and fled the stage. Arms and legs flew in all directions. The edge of a boot struck the glass podium holding the trophy. It toppled back and forth for a few precarious seconds, as if determined not to fall, but another escaping parent slammed into it with his full body, sealing its fate. The trophy flew from the stand and tumbled through the air, hitting the stage in a series of sickening thuds.

Mr. Eriksson spied their nearest exit and took charge. "Stay calm, everyone, and follow me."

Mom and Nanna Flo took Boo's hands while Dad held onto India.

Summer looked lost until India reached out. "Come with us."

Mr. Trifle held tight to Holly, and the Kapoors nestled Rajish between them.

The pandemonium of panic was only added to by the activation of the fire sprinklers.

Water sprayed over the entire room to frantic shrieks and cries. The television crew threw jackets on the cameras, and parents bundled their children to safety. Some slipped in puddles of water; others tripped over forgotten handbags.

A little girl fell in front of Mr. Eriksson and was in danger of being trampled. Grandpop held onto Peter while scooping her up with one arm.

As the crowd inched toward the doors, trying to stay on their feet and avoid flying elbows, India felt her anger rise. She

was sure that this was no accident. The banner, the destroyed dinner, the blackout, and now this—someone was behind these acts of malfeasance.

Of treachery.

Of chicanery.

When they reached the exit, India turned back to see Mr. O'Malley still onstage, his suit dripping with water, his silvery black hair plastered against his face, looking like a captain about to go down with his ship.

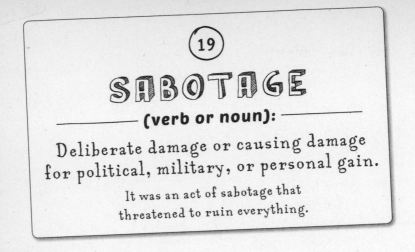

19

SABOTAGE

(verb or noun):

Deliberate damage or causing damage for political, military, or personal gain.

It was an act of sabotage that threatened to ruin everything.

"*CANCELED?*" NANNA FLO CRIED.

"That's what it says here."

It was much later, after the Wimples had gone back to their room and changed into dry clothes, that Boo saw a note had been slipped beneath their door.

"What a load of *piffle*! They can't just cancel the competition. These kids have worked too hard!"

If it was possible that a heart could sink, India's did just that. "What else does the note say?"

Boo read on. "It is with great sadness that, due to several misfortunes that have occurred during the opening days of the Most Marvelous International Spelling Bee, it has been decided, for the safety of all participants, to cancel the competition." Boo looked up. "I'm sorry, India."

"Who wrote the note?"

"It's signed Esmerelda Stomp."

"*Fiddle-faddle* and *balderdash*!" It was Nanna Flo again, and she was angry. "I'm going to go down there and give her a piece of my mind."

India sent a pleading look to Dad, worried that Nanna Flo may not be the best person to work things out. "Maybe it'll be better if I go with the other spellers?"

"That's a good idea," Dad agreed.

"He's right," Boo joined in. "It'll be more convincing coming from kids."

Nanna rolled up her sleeves. "Oh, I can be pretty convincing, believe me."

"You sure can," Mom said, "but it'll be harder to say no to kids."

Nanna still had her doubts. "All right, but the second you need me, you call."

India kissed Nanna Flo on the cheek. "I will."

India phoned the others, and they met in a secluded lounge area in the hotel lobby. They leaned in close so they wouldn't be overheard.

"Rajish is right," India began. "These *accidents* aren't accidents at all. I think they were meant to sabotage the bee so it'd be canceled."

"And it worked." Peter sighed.

"For now," India said. "But what if we discovered who's behind it? Then maybe the bee would go on."

Holly wondered where they'd even begin their search. "It could be anyone."

"Not just *anyone*," India said in a conspiratorial tone.

Rajish moved in even closer. "Who do you think it is?"

India waited a moment before she revealed her suspect. "Esmerelda Stomp."

"Why would the spelling bee director ruin her own bee?" Peter asked.

"Before our meeting yesterday, I met her in the elevator. She told me she didn't like spelling bees or kids and that she wouldn't mind if the competition was canceled."

"Someone's in the wrong job," Summer quipped.

"Also, the night the dogs ran through the Imperial Dining Hall, Esmerelda didn't help one bit and instead stood back, smiling, as if she were enjoying every minute."

"That doesn't prove she did it," Rajish said.

"I know, but it makes her a suspect."

"How do we prove it?" Holly asked.

Summer leaned her elbows on the table and clasped her hands in front of her lips, like a detective in a movie. "What if we got her to admit it? We could pay her a visit, distressed that the competition has been canceled and that all our dreams have been shattered."

"Go and see her?" Peter turned pale. "When?"

"Now," Summer decided. "Who's in?"

They all held up their hands. Except Peter.

"She seems kind of angry all the time."

"It'll be fine," India said. "We'll be together."

Prince Harry appeared from Peter's coat.

"You think I should go too, don't you?" The crested gecko poked out his tongue. "All right, I'm in too."

~~~~~

"I'm terribly sorry you feel that way," Esmerelda's voice said through her door, clearly irritated. "But if your daughter is that upset, I suggest calling room service and ordering a new box of tissues!"

Whatever small amount of patience Esmerelda had was clearly gone.

The five spellers stood outside her door. India threw back her shoulders, wriggled her fingers, and tried to ignore the increasing urge to run away.

She knocked.

The director's voice snarled from within. "What now?" Her footsteps thudded closer.

Peter slipped behind Summer.

Esmerelda wrenched the door open, her face puce with anger.

"See?" Peter whispered. "She's angry."

Prince Harry buried himself deep inside Peter's pocket.

"If you've come to complain about your ruined clothes, send your dry cleaning bills to hotel reception, and we'll pay for the damage." She was about to turn away when she added, "Oh, and we're sorry for any upset caused."

Esmerelda did not look sorry at all. Actually, she looked more like someone in need of a very long vacation.

"Now, I have to go. I'm very busy." She began to close the door.

"Ms. Stomp." India stuck her foot in the doorway.

Esmerelda scowled as if a muddy dog were trying to barge its way into her home.

"We're sorry to disturb you, but we wanted to tell you…" India found it hard to keep her voice steady with her heart beating so fast. "We think someone is behind all the accidents at the bee."

Esmerelda released the door and slowly crossed her arms. "Do you now?"

India wasn't sure exactly how Esmerelda did it, but she sounded even more unwelcoming than before.

"Yes." India knew she had to be careful. "And we were wondering… We wanted to ask…if it was you."

"*Me?*" The director moved closer, like a spider crawling toward a moth trapped in its web. "What makes you think it was me?"

India gulped. She glanced at Rajish, who gave her an encouraging nod. "When I first met you in the elevator, you told me that you didn't like spelling bees or kids and that you wouldn't mind if the bee was canceled."

"That's true." She loomed even closer, her jaw clenched. "What else?"

"When the dogs ruined the dinner, you stood back and smiled, as if you were enjoying every minute."

She nodded. "That's true too. I was enjoying it very much."

Holly was puzzled. "So you did it?"

"I don't believe in dog shows and dressing up animals to be something they're not. When I saw those dogs chasing that cat, I was happy because that's how dogs are *supposed* to act—not prancing about with ribbons in their fur. It's been the highlight of all the spelling bees so far."

"So you didn't do it?" Holly was still trying to decipher what Esmerelda was saying.

"Of course not," Esmerelda insisted. "It's true I'm not fond of children—or adults for that matter—but I'd never sabotage the bee to avoid them. I agree that the 'accidents' were cleverly disguised attempts to ruin everything, but what I also know is that the venue is no longer safe. That's why the bee has been canceled and Mr. O'Malley has been fired."

"Fired?" India was having trouble believing what Esmerelda was saying.

"Of course. Mr. O'Malley swore an oath to the Queen that as her representative, he would make sure the bee ran without a hitch, and he has failed miserably."

"But he loved the competition," Peter argued.

"Not enough to do his job properly, and he's left a giant mess, which I now have to clean up. I knew we should have given the position to Mr. Harrington. He applied too, but the Queen wanted Mr. O'Malley. She was insistent."

"Where is Mr. O'Malley now?" India asked.

Esmerelda looked as if she had a million other things she'd rather be doing than answering annoying questions. "Hotel security has taken him to his room so he can pack his things and be removed from the property. Now, if you'll excuse me, I've had my fill of whiny children for today."

India pulled her leg out of the way just in time for the door to slam shut. A lock clicked into place.

No one moved. India stared at the door, trying to make sense of what she'd just heard. "We have to find Mr. O'Malley before he leaves."

They ran to the elevator and hurried to his room. When they got there, his door was slightly ajar. India knocked softly. "Mr. O'Malley, may we come in?"

"Yes," a weak voice floated from inside.

Two burly security guards looked on as a disheveled Mr. O'Malley gathered his things and dropped them into his suitcase. His hair had dried but was in a tangled mess. He was wearing mismatched socks, and his shirt was wrinkled and untucked over a pair of gray sweat pants.

"Mr. O'Malley," India said. "We've just spoken to Esmerelda."

"Ah." He slipped his silk cravats from their hangers and tossed them into his bag. "So you know."

India hoped he would tell her it wasn't true, that he knew who was behind the accidents and that he would fix everything, that they shouldn't worry about a thing because the spelling bee would continue with him at the helm.

But he said none of that.

"I have been fired"—the wrinkles on his faces deepened—"for incompetence." The energy seemed to drain from him, and he sank onto the bed. "I love the spelling bee, and my job as the Queen's representative is the most magnificent privilege of my life." For a brief moment, he smiled, until misery swooped in and stole it away again. "At least it was."

"It's not fair!" Summer jammed her fists into her hips.

"None of the accidents were your fault," Peter chimed in.

"My job was to make sure everything ran smoothly." Mr. O'Malley looked as if he could barely lift his head. "And it most certainly did not."

India felt a rush of sadness at the sight of Mr. O'Malley. "There's obviously someone behind this."

Holly felt it too. "But instead of catching them, they fire you."

"I'm sorry to say," Rajish said, "it doesn't make any sense."

"I appreciate your kindness, I truly do, but it is only right that

I get sent away. But the Queen—I've worked with her for years." A tear quivered on his eyelash, fell, and splashed onto his hands. "She trusted me, and now she'll want nothing to do with me."

One of the guards looked at his watch. "We're sorry, Mr. O'Malley, but it's time to go."

"Of course, Hector." He closed his suitcase and lifted it from the bed. He stroked the royal crest on his suit, which he'd neatly laid out on the couch. "Please ensure this is sent back to the palace."

The guards nodded keenly and led Mr. O'Malley from the room. The children followed in silence and took the elevator to the lobby, where he was escorted to a waiting taxi.

"It has been a pleasure meeting you, children." Mr. O'Malley recovered a trace of his former, more confident self. "You are a true inspiration."

He took one last look at the Royal Windsor Hotel and stepped into the shadowy interior of the cab. As they drove away, his head fell, and his shoulders shook. India had simply never seen anyone so miserable in her whole short life.

And she was going to do something about it.

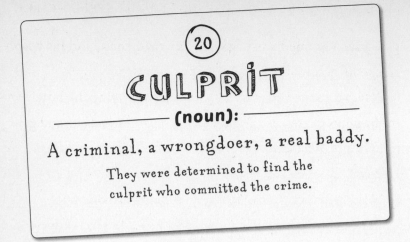

20

CULPRIT

(noun):

A criminal, a wrongdoer, a real baddy.

They were determined to find the culprit who committed the crime.

INDIA SHIVERED WITH FURY AS she watched Mr. O'Malley's taxi disappear into the snarl of traffic. "We need to find out who sabotaged the bee."

"How?" Holly asked.

"We'll find proof of the real culprit."

"Maybe we can help."

India turned to see the security guards who had ushered Mr. O'Malley out. They were tall, muscular, and wore name badges saying "Hector" and "Carlos."

"We have been at the Royal Windsor Hotel for more than nineteen years." Hector's long mustache wriggled as he spoke, and his eyes had the gleam of a fan. "I've worked with many people, and Mr. O'Malley is a true gentleman."

Carlos slammed a fist against his broad chest, and his voice cracked with emotion. "He was like a brother."

"He has looked after us very well. In preparing the hotel for the bee, he ordered us special dinners if we worked late and gave us presents of handmade royal chocolates. They were *delicioso*," Hector said.

"*Muy delicioso!*" Carlos swayed his bald head dreamily.

"The ones with the hazelnuts were the best," Hector decided.

"No, no, no." Carlos shook his stubby finger at his friend. "The best were the ones with the tiny dried cherries."

"*¿Estas loco?*" Hector slapped his forehead. "The best were the—"

"You can help us prove he didn't do it?" Rajish was keen to get them back on the subject of Mr. O'Malley.

"*Sí.*" Hector searched either side of him and lowered his voice. "We have access to the security footage from all the cameras in the hotel. If we look closely, maybe we'll find a clue."

"But it will take many eyes." Carlos nodded with cool composure.

Hector and Carlos held their heads high, as if posing for a calendar of World's Best Security Guards.

India and Rajish swapped confused glances. "Do you think we can see the footage?" India asked.

"*Absolutamente!*" Hector cried. "Follow us."

The guards led the way through a labyrinth of corridors in the hotel's interior to the security room. It was small and dark and lined with a network of monitors.

Hector stuck his thumbs in his belt and hitched his pants higher. "This is the heart of the Royal Windsor. If anything sneaky has happened, we will find it here."

"There will be no escape for the person who did this." Carlos slammed a fist into his hand. "We need to be tough and fearless and..."

Prince Harry climbed out of Peter's pocket and onto his shoulder.

"Aah!" Despite Carlos's size, he jumped into Hector's arms.

"He won't hurt you," Peter said and patted Prince Harry to prove it. "He doesn't like to miss out."

Hector placed Carlos back on the ground, making sure he was OK. "*Bueno?*"

"*Sí, bueno, gracias.*" Carlos

moved away from the scaly creature. "I watched *Godzilla* as a kid and had nightmares for years."

They each sat in front of a monitor, and Hector explained how to operate the equipment. "Watch for anything unusual or anyone acting suspiciously."

They examined the black-and-white footage. Most of it was of empty corridors, kitchens full of chopping and stirring, or the main lobby bustling with guests, hotel staff wheeling carts of luggage or cakes, and dog owners grooming pooches.

It was tedious. It was monotonous.

Until Holly noticed something unusual.

"I think I've found something," she said.

Everyone gathered around. "This is the kitchen the night before the dinner."

They saw the chef take one last look around before he turned off the light. The room was thrown into darkness, apart from the green glow of the exit signs.

Holly fast-forwarded the footage before pressing Play.

"There!" Holly's excitement was heightened by the blue glow of the screen. "See?"

The others squinted, trying to find what she'd spotted.

She pointed at the corner of the screen. "Here! You can see

movement." It was like watching a shadow within a shadow. "Someone's there."

"I can see it!" Peter said.

It was subtle, but someone was definitely there.

"Watch what happens next." Holly peered at the screen with mounting anticipation.

The tall, thin figure disappeared for a few moments before he reappeared in the glow of the exit sign.

But this time, he was carrying something.

As he opened the door to leave, light from outside splashed over him, lighting up his face and the item he was holding.

"It's a can of food," India said. "Can we zoom in?"

Hector enlarged the image until they saw the tin and the intruder's face more clearly.

Holly raised an eyebrow. "Well, surprise, surprise."

Peter shared her delight. "Gravy powder."

"*Fantastico!*" Hector twirled his mustache.

"*Muy fantastico!*" Carlos seemed more relaxed now that he was nowhere near Prince Harry.

"I've seen that man," Summer realized. "In the hotel lobby on the day we arrived. He was standing beside a housekeeping cart, and I asked him if the hotel had pink sheets, because they're my favorite, but he said he didn't know, and I asked him how he could work at the hotel and not know such an important detail, but he raised an eyebrow and walked away."

"How terrible for you. Were you OK?" Rajish offered Summer a sympathetic hand, which she met with a raised eyebrow.

"I had a long bath to recover."

India found footage of the lobby from two days earlier. It was brimming with guests and staff.

"That's him." Summer pointed to a man wearing a long coat with a hat drawn low over his face. "He's the only person not moving, and he's looking up."

"Let me guess," Rajish said. "It's only moments before the banner falls."

At that very second, that was exactly what happened.

"Yes," India said. "And everyone in the lobby is suitably shocked—except for him."

The man in the coat offered a smug, knowing smile before pulling up his collar and casually leaving the hotel.

"It's hard to see his face in that hat," Rajish said. "How can we be sure it's him?"

"The ring." Summer pointed to the image from the kitchen. "There's a skull ring on his pinkie finger. Here and"—she pointed to India's screen—"here."

"Who notices a ring?" Peter asked.

"I do," Summer said. "Everyone knows a skull ring is a fashion disaster."

"Keep looking." India was more determined than ever to find out if this was their man. "I bet we'll find more evidence."

Buoyed by their findings so far, they searched further, scrutinizing every frame on every monitor, when suddenly Peter cried, "There he is again!" In a dimly lit corridor, they saw a man dressed in a sweat suit and cap. "Watch what he's holding behind his back."

The man looked all around before opening a door and disappearing inside…with a set of wire cutters. And this time, they clearly saw his face.

"Where does that door lead?" Rajish asked.

Hector double-checked the number on the monitor. "It's the rear entrance to the Heritage Ballroom."

Peter read the time code on the video. "Seven forty-five in the evening. When was the blackout?"

"Just before eight," Carlos said. "I know because I was supposed to finish at eight, but they asked us to stay on after the trouble for extra security."

Summer leaned closer to the screen. "Can we see his face again?"

Peter rewound the footage and stopped it the second the figure turned to the camera. This time, his face could be clearly seen.

"He's the waiter who spilled water on Holly's mom during the dinner."

"I've got that footage." Rajish rewound the footage. Various angles of the ballroom flashed on his screen. "That's him!" He pressed pause on the image of a waiter serving dinner.

"And there's the skull ring." Summer shivered at the thought of it. "How does anyone even *think* that's OK to wear?"

"Do you know who that man is?" Rajish asked Hector and Carlos.

"I can check the hotel's staff list." Carlos moved to his computer and began flicking through security photos of all the employees. He scrolled past each one until he found a match.

"Reko Nelson." Carlos read his details. "He's been here for three weeks."

"People..." Summer wasn't ready to drop the detective act. "Looks like we have our man."

India felt her heart quicken. "Can you find out when he's working next?"

Carlos looked through the rosters; his face slowly brightened. "He is here now, preparing the Imperial Dining Hall for a special dinner."

Hector straightened his tie. "Not for long, because we are about to pay him a visit. *Vámonos*, Carlos."

Within ten minutes, Carlos and Hector entered the control room with Reko Nelson firmly wedged between them.

He balked at the sight of the spellers standing by the screens. "We have company, I see."

"Please," Hector said as he pulled out a chair, "have a seat."

"Will this take long?" Reko flashed a smile that reeked of confidence. "I have to get back to work."

"Not long." Carlos gripped Reko's shoulders with more than a little force than was friendly. "These children just have a few questions they would like to ask." He slapped Reko's back before folding his arms and nodding at India. "He's all yours."

"In the last few days, there have been a series of accidents at this hotel," India began.

"Yes, I heard." Reko shook his head in mock sympathy. "There's been quite a lot of bad luck going around."

"Bad luck?" Holly said. "We think they were more deliberate than bad luck."

"Deliberate?" Reko feigned shock. "That's terrible, but I've got to get back to—" Reko tried to stand, but Carlos's hands again landed on his puny shoulders.

"You're not going anywhere," Carlos said with a smiling sneer.

"Not anywhere," Hector repeated in a low, menacing voice.

"Ready everyone?" India asked.

The spellers spun their chairs toward the monitors. "Ready."

One by one, they showed Reko the footage, explaining their sabotage theory. With each incident, his cocky smile was whittled away.

Reko glanced behind him. The hulking bodies of Hector and Carlos stood before the door, blocking any chance of escape.

"Why did you do it?" Holly asked.

"Money."

"You ruined an international spelling competition for money?" India again felt her anger rise.

"It was more than I could earn in a year," he argued.

"Who paid you?" Rajish asked.

"Why should I tell?" He snorted.

"Because at the moment," Hector said, hovering close to his ear, "you're going to take the blame for all this."

Carlos hissed quietly into his other ear. "And possibly go to jail."

"Oh." Strangely, this didn't seem to have occurred to Reko. "But they were just a few harmless pranks."

"Harmless pranks!" Now it was Summer's turn to get mad. She paced the room, doing a very good impersonation of a lawyer about to argue her case. "Oh no, my friend, you have broken quite a few laws. There's malicious damage of property, intentionally endangering human life, cruelty to animals, and, most importantly"—she was only inches away from Reko's face—"recklessly threatening to damage haute couture."

Reko was confused. "Haute couture?"

"That was an Armani dress I was wearing at dinner." Summer sat down and flicked her hair over her shoulders. "Best guess is five years in prison before you get parole. If you confess, the judge is likely to be more lenient."

Reko laughed. "Five years? In *prison*? What would you know? You're just a kid."

"With parents who are two of Australia's top lawyers. Didn't I mention that?"

What little confidence Reko had finally dripped away, much like the color in his face.

"If I confess," he said quietly, desperately trying to figure out his next move, "it'll be better for me?"

"Oh yes, much better."

Reko's voice lost all its spark. "It was Harrington Hathaway."

For a few moments, no one said anything, mostly because it was exactly the opposite of what they had expected to hear.

"The spelling bee champion?" India said in disbelief.

"That's the guy."

"But why?" Rajish, like the others, was finding it hard to take in.

"He never said. He wanted me to mess things up a little—not hurt anyone, just ruin the bee for someone, and then he would pay me. Handsomely."

"Someone who? One of the contestants? A parent? The Queen?"

"I don't know, but whoever it is, he has a real grudge against them."

"Come on." Hector lifted Reko to his feet with one hand like he were made of straw. "We're going to Ms. Stomp's room so you can tell her the truth."

Carlos put his hand on his heart. "Nice work, *mis amigos*."

They shuffled a deflated Reko from the room.

Summer quickly reached into her pocket for her phone. "Wait until Mr. O'Malley finds out we have evidence that will clear his name." She bit her lip and waited until he finally answered. "Mr. O'Malley, it's Summer. We have good news. We know who caused the accidents at the bee."

The others shared looks of glee.

"It was a waiter at the hotel, and you are not going to believe this, but he was paid by Harrington Hathaway. He was doing it to make someone look bad, but we don't know who."

There was another pause. Summer's excitement slowly faded. "Oh."

The others stared as she kept listening.

"Of course," she said. "We'll meet you there."

"What did he say?" India was confused. Mr. O'Malley should have been ecstatic, but that's not what seemed to have happened at all.

"He wants to meet us at Café Mistero across the road from the hotel. He says he knows why Harrington did it."

"Why?" Holly asked.

"Because of something that happened a very long time ago."

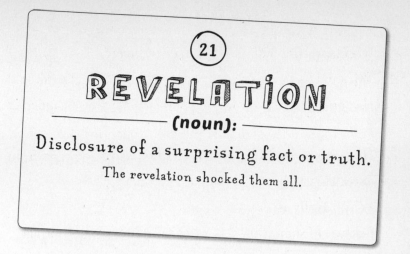

21

REVELATION

(noun):

Disclosure of a surprising fact or truth.
The revelation shocked them all.

IN A COZY BOOTH IN the far corner of Café Mistero, Mr. O'Malley and the five spellers gathered beneath a dim overhead light. Their mugs of hot chocolate released steam into the air, as if their collective gloom had risen up between them.

"A long time ago," Mr. O'Malley began, stirring the melting marshmallow in his cup, "when I was a young boy, I lived in a small house in a coal-mining town called Bogstow. I was short and wore pants pulled up high to my waist. And I could spell. Brilliantly. Much like you all."

He smiled briefly.

"I lived with my mom, dad, and twin baby brothers. We didn't have much money, and there were times when my parents went without food to make sure we never went hungry. I loved visiting the library, which I did most afternoons, but one particular day, I saw a poster calling for entrants for a national spelling bee.

"I read the poster again and again, memorizing all the details, especially the part about the five hundred dollars in prize money. I wondered what so much money would look like. I imagined a pile of bills reaching higher than our house, higher than Cragg's Hill, the highest part of all Bogstow.

"I raced all the way home through the coal-dusted alleys, through sheets of gray, flapping laundry. I knew this was the moment our lives would change forever. I could *feel* it.

"The day of the first round, I was so nervous, I could barely stand. The pronouncer called me to the microphone three times before I finally convinced my brain to move my legs. After four hours, countless words, and a lot of hand-wringing, it was over."

"You won?" Holly was literally on the edge of her seat.

Mr. O'Malley nodded. "I did. I won the next few rounds until I found myself invited to compete in the grand final. Mom and Dad used all their savings to send me to London, and I knew I had to win for them."

Mr. O'Malley smiled, remembering the details of a moment long ago.

"When I handed my parents the money, my dad cried. He said

he didn't think there were two parents who'd ever felt prouder. Then came the invitation for the international competition. My family helped me practice every day. My mom sewed me a new pair of pants, and my grandma bought me a new jacket—the first one I'd ever owned."

"And you won," Peter guessed.

"No." Mr. O'Malley looked down, gripping his mug of chocolate. "I made it through the final round, but on the night before the grand final, the director's room was broken into." He winced, as if the next part were too painful to say out loud. "And the cards for round two were found in my room."

"But you didn't take them." India knew Mr. O'Malley's revelation was untrue.

"No. I would never cheat. It was Harrington. He even admitted it."

Rajish rankled at the injustice. "Why didn't you tell the director?"

"Harrison told me if I did, he'd deny everything," Mr. O'Malley said. "I was a poor boy from a coal mining town, Harrington was rich, and his father was one of the spelling bee sponsors. I knew no one would believe me.

"I was banned forever from competing. Worse than that, it broke my mother's heart—she never looked at me the same way again."

"We're going to see him," India decided.

"I agree," Rajish said without hesitation.

"Really?" Peter shifted in his seat. "Because he sounds pretty nasty."

"He can't get away with it," Summer argued. "Not again."

"He'll never admit it," Mr. O'Malley said.

"He has to." India had never felt more resolved about anything in her life. "We're going to his house, and I'm going to make him."

"I don't want to be mean," Summer said carefully, "but *you*?"

"Yes." India frowned. "Why not me?"

"Because we want a cheat and a liar to invite us into his home so he can confess to a crime, and you're too... nice." She flicked her head back. "This is going to take special skills—skills built up over years by someone always determined to get her way."

"Meaning you?"

"Yes, me."

"She was very good back there with Reko," Rajish reasoned.

"And that wasn't even my best work," Summer bragged. "Who votes that I be the one to make Harrington confess?"

Rajish, Peter, and Summer slowly raised their hands.

Holly paused for a moment before raising hers too. "Sorry, India."

"Good choice, everyone." Summer turned to Mr. O'Malley. "Do you have his number?"

"Of course." He retrieved Harrington's details from his phone.

Summer entered the numbers and put the call on speaker.

"Harrington Hathaway the Third speaking. How may I improve your life?"

"Mr. Hathaway, my name is Summer Millicent Ernestine Beauregard-Champion, and I am calling from the Harrington Hathaway Fan Club."

"I have a fan club?" Harrington was clearly impressed.

"Oh yes! We have quite a few members who are all *tremendous* fans."

"Well, that is very flattering."

"It's nothing more than you deserve, Mr. Hathaway." She paused, building up to her next comment. "You are our hero. My friends and I are from the Most Marvelous International Spelling Bee, which sadly has been canceled due to a series of unfortunate accidents."

Summer listened carefully, but he responded without a hint of guilt. "Terrible business indeed."

India gave Summer an irritated look, but the interrogator had only just started and wasn't fazed at all.

"We are, understandably, heartbroken," she continued, "but what would help mend our young and delicate hearts is the chance to meet you and have your autograph."

"Well now, little lady, I am a very busy man—"

"Please, Mr. Hathaway, it would go such a long way to alleviating our devastation."

"I understand it is upsetting, but I—"

"When I saw you at the spelling bee dinner," Summer said, actually sounding as if she were crying, "you changed my life."

"I did?"

"Absolutely. I knew I had finally found someone I could look up to for the rest of my life. And I wasn't alone. It would mean the world to us to hear from the greatest spelling champion of all time."

There was a pause. India crossed her fingers.

"Well, I suppose I could spare a few minutes, for the edification and consolation of the young. When shall I expect you?"

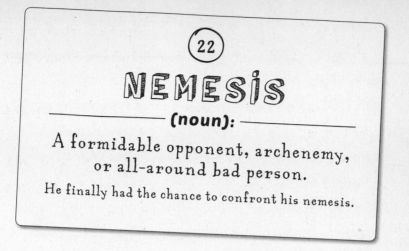

22

NEMESIS

(noun):

A formidable opponent, archenemy, or all-around bad person.

He finally had the chance to confront his nemesis.

"THIS IS YOUR CAR?"

Peter nestled into the leather seats of the limousine, positive he was the only one in his family ever to have done so.

"Yes, when we're in London." Summer was sitting opposite Peter and wasn't sure why he was so shocked. "Mommy and Daddy let me use it whenever I need it, and Hansen has been driving me places since I was a baby. Haven't you, Hansen?"

"Yes, Miss Summer." The stony-faced driver replied without missing a beat.

Peter stared as they passed street after street of multistoried mansions sprawling behind ornate iron gates. The afternoon was fading, and one by one, lights turned on, sending out an almost fairy-tale glow over the hedges, stately balconies, and bubbling fountains. "Harrington must have some serious money to live in this neighborhood."

"He is very wealthy," Mr. O'Malley said. "After winning the international spelling bee three times in a row—a feat no one else has ever repeated—he was hailed as a child genius."

"It helps when you're a cheat." Holly scowled.

"After that, Harrington set up his first tutoring company when he was still a teenager, promising to produce child geniuses just like himself. The classes were a worldwide success, and he became even wealthier."

India felt her whole body burn with anger. "While you were accused of something you didn't do."

"Don't worry." Summer dug out a hairbrush from the seat-back pocket in front of her and ran it through her hair. "After we play the adoring fans, he'll admit what he's done."

"Please be careful," Mr. O'Malley said. "He has a terrible temper."

"He does?" Peter was worried. "Maybe we could get him to confess by phone instead."

Summer replaced the brush and sat up with renewed determination. "Follow my lead, and everything will be fine."

Peter wondered how people like Summer did it—how they had so much confidence when he had almost none. He stared out the window, the lights from the mansions playing across his face.

"Mr. Harrington's home is coming up on the left, Miss Summer," Hansen said.

Rajish gave Mr. O'Malley an apologetic look. "It's time to hide."

"Good luck," Mr. O'Malley said as he crouched on the limousine floor. "And thank you."

Summer took a shawl from the armrest beside her and placed it over him. "Just to be safe."

"We won't be long," India said. "I promise."

Summer took out her phone. "I'm going to call you now and keep the call going so you can hear everything we're saying."

Mr. O'Malley answered immediately, and Summer dropped her phone in her pocket. "And we're ready."

Hansen pulled up at the gates, which were fashioned into a golden *H*. Strings of lights flickered around the edges like the entrance to a theme park.

The driver announced their arrival into the intercom. The gates swung slowly open, splitting the *H* in two. They drove down the tree-lined driveway that was lit on either side by smaller *H*-shaped lights. The sprawling mansion soon towered above them.

Hansen pulled up, and the children climbed out of the limousine. There was something about the size and easy magnificence of the building that made Peter feel very, very small. "It's like a palace."

A man in a long, dark coat with gold trim and white gloves appeared on the front veranda. "Mr. Harrington is ready to see you."

They followed him inside between two life-size gold statues of Harrington.

"It's good to have a healthy ego, I guess," Rajish muttered.

Holly treaded lightly down the long corridor that was lined with paintings, some of them very famous. "A Van Gogh," she said in awe. "He owns a Van Gogh."

They were shown into a light-filled drawing room with marble stands bearing trophies and medals and walls plastered with photographs of Harrington as a boy receiving awards from pronouncers and world leaders. There was even one with the Queen.

At the head of the room was Harrington himself, seated on a gold, throne-like chair. "How lovely for you to meet with me."

He was dressed in a red velvet robe tied with a golden cord. India thought the only thing that was missing was a crown. She clenched her jaw at the sight of his smug, smiling face. She wished she had brought Nanna Flo with her. Nanna was never one to tolerate superiority and self-importance and would have given him something to be sorry about. But if Summer was miffed, she didn't let it show one bit.

"It is such an honor to be in your presence, Mr. Hathaway."

She reached out and shook his hand. "This is simply one of the greatest moments of my life."

Harrington blushed. "It is always a thrill to encountenance one's idols."

"It's more than a thrill." Summer was in her element. "It's a privilege I will remember for the rest of my life."

"Please," Harrington said, clearly enjoying the admiration, "have a seat."

The children sat down on an antique chaise longue opposite his throne. Behind Harrington were glass doors that overlooked a sprawling but finely manicured garden. Peter scowled at the lake in the center until he realized it was actually a fountain, and in the middle was a statue of Harrington himself. Lit from below, he was holding a book in one hand and a trophy in the other, with water spouting from both.

"Would you mind if we recorded you?" Holly carried out the role of adoring fan with great skill. "It'll be a souvenir we can keep forever."

"I'd rather you didn't—"

"I will play it every morning, so I can hear your wisdom and try to be more like you."

"Even though we'll never have your natural intelligence," Rajish added.

As much as it irritated India even *pretending* to like this man, she knew they needed to act as a team if their plan was going to work. "No," she said as she shook her head sadly, "but it will give us something to strive for."

"Well," Harrington chuckled, "it's humbling to know I have made your lives so meaningful."

"How did you feel when you won your first international spelling bee?" Summer asked.

"Well, *that* was a *great* day." He crossed his legs and shook his silver mane of hair. "I was nervous, of course, but in the end, the best speller won."

"What tips do you have for those who aspire to be like you?" Holly asked with bright-eyed curiosity.

Harrington settled happily into his throne. India got the feeling he sat there quite a lot. "It's the big three: hard work, practice, and a natural, innate talent."

"You must have competed against some tough rivals," Summer said.

"There were other admirable spellers, but no one I couldn't out-spell when the time came."

"We heard Mr. O'Malley was a brilliant speller too," Holly said as innocently as she could.

Harrington flinched before he regained his composure. "Was he?"

"He competed against you when you won your third international competition." India shuffled forward. "You must remember him."

"There were so many children, I—"

"Yes, but only three spellers from the same country make it to the international competition. You and he were two of them."

He pulled at a loose thread on his robe. "I was very focused, which is the motto of my company—*Stay Focused, Be Successful.*" He rubbed his hands. "Which reminds me, I should get back to it."

Summer waited a few moments before she delivered her next line. "But we haven't even had time to chat about Reko."

Harrington's head snapped toward her. "*Reko?*" His voice sounded strangled.

"He's a waiter at the hotel. He had lots of interesting things to say about you." She frowned and tapped her chin. "What were they again?"

Harrington was desperate to change the subject. "Shall I sign your autograph books before you leave?"

"I remember." India had never considered becoming an actress, but she impressed herself by her fake remembering. "He told us about the cat he dunked in gravy. You know, the one that ran through the Imperial Dining Hall and caused such chaos."

"Yes!" Holly cried. "And he also mentioned tampering with the ropes on the banner, and the wire cutters he used to cause the blackout."

"He sounds thoroughly unpleasant." Harrison shifted uncomfortably in his throne, as if it were suddenly lined with tacks. "You'd be wise to have nothing to do with him."

Rajish looked at his watch. "Esmerelda Stomp should know all about it by now too."

"There was something else he told us." Summer was getting ready for her big finale. "Something about being paid."

"Yes!" India let her cry hover in the air for a few moments before adding, "Something about being paid by *you.*"

"What... I never... That's *outrageous*," Harrington sputtered. "The lengths people will go to to destroy the rich and famous are—"

"He said you did it to ruin the bee for someone." Rajish fixed him with an accusatory eye.

Harrington stood up and tightened the cord on his robe. "I'm going to have to ask you to leave. I'm very busy."

"It was Mr. O'Malley, wasn't it?" Summer's words were like a blow to his stomach.

"Mr. O'Malley?" Harrington huffed. "Why would I want to harm Mr. O'Malley?"

"Because," India began with some delight, "he is a brilliant speller who you thought would ruin your chances at becoming the first three-time world champion."

"And you deliberately planted spelling bee cards in his room so he'd be expelled for cheating," Rajish added.

"You children have the most active imaginations." His voice was riddled with menace. "You ought to be careful they don't get you into trouble. Now, I really must ask you—"

"And you sabotaged him again *this* year." Summer wasn't about to be dissuaded, menacing voice or not. "Because you requested to be the Queen's representative, and she turned you down."

"She preferred Mr. O'Malley over you," Holly finished with a broad smile.

Harrington's body stiffened. His hands opened and closed into fists.

"It should have been *me. I'm* the champion. I'm the one who deserved the Queen's attention, not a cheat and a liar like O'Malley." He was seething now, the anger churning in him like a boiling kettle. "Not that…that…*namby-pamby.*"

The children smiled, knowing Harrington had as good as admitted it was him—and they had it all recorded.

The only one not smiling was Peter.

And it was because of those two words: *namby-pamby.*

Words that were thrown at him on the bus and in the playground. Words used as weapons during sports and to turn his friends against him. Words hurled at him, letting him know he was worthless—and he always would be.

And those words had worked.

Until now.

Hearing them again, used against someone else, made Peter's back straighten and his fear fall away. Before Harrington could say anything more, Peter was on his feet. He stepped forward, pointing a finger at the flaming, bloated face of Harrington Hathaway the Third.

"You're nothing but a bully. A sad, empty, rich man who wants nothing more than to be adored, and you do it by making others feel small—others who can't stand up for themselves when they should. Mr. O'Malley is a good man who is kinder, smarter, and more loyal than you'll ever be."

Harrington was rigid with anger. He took one small, threatening step toward Peter. "Is that so?" His voice was dangerously low.

Peter recognized in Harrington's face the same look in his eyes, the same turned up lip as when Bruiser loomed over him.

But this time, the bullying wasn't going to work.

India and the others moved to Peter's side.

"Yeah." He felt bolstered by them just being there. "That's so."

The air was charged with Harrington's quiet rage. Then a strange thing happened: he sank back into his throne, defeated.

"OK," he sighed.

"*OK*? You mean you did it?" Holly made sure to keep her phone out of sight, in case he ordered her to stop recording.

"I never meant to hurt anyone. I just wanted to ruin things a little."

"*Ruin* things a little?" Summer exclaimed. "You *ruined* several of my brand-new designer dresses!"

"I think what Summer meant," India said pointedly, "is that people could have been hurt."

"Well, of course, there's that too," Summer admitted.

"To think my dad wanted me to be like you." Rajish's glare was cold.

"He did?" It seemed only then that Harrington realized what he'd done.

"How could you?" came an unexpected voice from the back of the room.

"Elwood?" The color drained from Harrington's face when he saw Mr. O'Malley at the door.

The butler scurried in behind him. "Sorry, sir. He barged in."

Harrington waved him off. "What are you doing here?"

"I'm with them." Mr. O'Malley held up his phone. "And I heard every word."

"Oh."

"They're just kids," Mr. O'Malley said. "You did this to *them* to ruin *me*?"

"It wasn't supposed to be like that. I never meant to…"

All of Harrington's excuses melted away.

"When I discovered the Queen needed a new representative for the bee, I knew there'd be no greater endorsement for my business. I was the champion, but she chose you instead. I thought if I messed things up and made you look incompetent, she'd realize she'd made a mistake and give the position to me."

"Instead, the competition is canceled, and no one wins," India said.

Mr. O'Malley frowned. "All those years ago, you were a superlative speller. You probably would have won instead of me."

"I had to make sure," Harrington said.

"Why?" India asked. "When you'd already won twice?"

"My dad was a famous soccer player. He'd broken many records. To him, life was all about winning and being the best. I grew up in a house full of his trophies and medals. I wasn't any good at sports, much to his disappointment, but I was determined to make him proud. When I heard about the spelling bee, I knew that was how I could do it." Harrington smiled. "It took a lot of hard work—I practiced every chance I got—and I won two international finals. But it had been done before. I knew I needed to win one more to truly impress him. Then I came up against Elwood. He was a natural and had a knack for spelling words I'd never seen before. I had to make sure he wouldn't win."

"So you planted the cards in his room?" India asked.

"Not me, of course. I couldn't risk being caught. Not the son of the great *Harold Hathaway*." Harrington laughed, a sad, ironic laugh. "It's surprising how easily some people can be bought off."

India had heard enough. "We have to tell Esmerelda and

convince her to let the bee go on as scheduled." She turned away until she remembered one last thing. "Oh, and by the way, Mr. Hathaway, there's no such word as *encountenance*."

They hurried from the room, leaving Harrington hunched over in his throne, in his very large mansion, surrounded by his trophies and medals.

They scrambled into the limousine, and Holly immediately sent the recording she'd made. "Once Esmerelda hears this, she'll have to let the bee continue."

"Thank you," Mr. O'Malley said, teary eyed. "All of you."

"You're welcome." India looked quite pleased with herself. "It was time everyone knew the truth, and someone had to put a stop to Harrington's bullying."

"Which Peter did!" Holly said, nudging him with her elbow.

The crested gecko climbed out of Peter's pocket and leaped into his hands. Peter stroked his back.

India laughed. "Prince Harry thinks so too."

"You really stood up to him." Rajish patted Peter on the back.

"And with style." Summer sat opposite Peter, her arms folded, nodding in admiration. "I didn't know you had it in you."

"Neither did I," Peter confessed with a laugh. His heart hadn't quite settled since he'd left Harrington's mansion. "It felt good, but I couldn't have done it without you all there."

"We were like the three musketeers," Holly said. "Except there are five of us…and we're not musketeers."

Rajish held out his hand. "All for one!"

The others stacked their hands on top of his, one after the other. "And one for all."

Peter held Prince Harry in the air until the gecko bounded onto the pile of hands.

"Sorry," Holly apologized. "The six musketeers."

"Now that we've dealt with Mr. O'Malley's nemesis," Summer said, "let's make sure this spelling bee goes ahead. I've bought a dress especially for the finals, and the whole trip's going to be a *disaster* if I don't get to wear it."

"I think you mean we've worked so hard to be here that it would be a shame not to compete," India suggested.

Summer flicked her blond locks over her shoulder and wore an imperturbable smile. "That too."

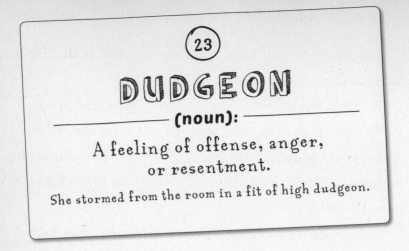

WHEN THEY ARRIVED AT THE Royal Windsor Hotel,
Esmerelda was waiting for them, her face a sickly shade of gray.
She'd been pacing the lobby, her clipboard gripped to her chest
as if it were a life jacket.

"Mr. O'Malley," she said with a quiver in her voice. "I've spoken
to Reko and watched the footage from Holly. I am truly sorry
and would like to invite you back as the Queen's representative."

"It would be my absolute pleasure," Mr. O'Malley said before
nervously adding, "And the Queen?"

"She knows everything and is more than relieved to have
you back."

A bright glow seemed to fill his whole body. He stood taller
and tried to smooth out his sweat suit. "As am I."

"What will happen to Harrington?" India asked.

The icy expression on Esmerelda's face said it all. "He is being dealt with."

"And the grand final?" Peter was almost too scared to ask.

"Will be going ahead tomorrow." There was a note of relief in Esmerelda's voice, followed quickly by her usual no-nonsense tone. "Which means we have a lot of work to do. Ready, Mr. O'Malley?"

Even though he was in his sweats and crumpled shirt, his hair a curly, unkempt mess, Mr. O'Malley somehow resumed a regal air. "Ready, Ms. Stomp."

The two were headed for the elevators, locked in deep discussion, when a screeching voice tore through the lobby.

"Where is she? I demand you find her now!"

It was Mrs. Trifle, who eventually laid eyes on her daughter. She strode across the lobby in a sparkly pink leotard with *Beaut Butts and Guts* emblazoned in sequins across her chest. "Where have you been?"

"I'm sorry." Holly wasn't sure where to start. "But we have some great news."

Mrs. Trifle continued as if Holly hadn't spoken. "I've been looking for you for over an hour."

"I know you must have been worried, but—"

"Worried? Of course I was—worried you were ruining a

life-changing opportunity that *I'd* created! We had an important interview set up with the BBC to talk about our fitness center—"

"And about Holly," Mr. Trifle said, finally catching up to his wife.

"But now it's not going to happen, because you were nowhere to be found, and we've missed our chance."

"Sorry, but we had to do something very important, which means the grand final is going to happen!"

"It was the BBC!" Her mother simply wasn't listening.

"I'm sorry." Holly cowered before her mother's blotchy red face.

Peter's heart quickened. It was the third time Holly had said sorry, but this didn't seem to do anything to calm down Mrs. Trifle. If anything, it seemed to make her angrier.

Prince Harry poked his nose out of Peter's jacket. He'd been woken by the pounding of Peter's heart, but he was also hungry, and there was a smell—something delicious and beefy.

And it was coming from Mr. Trifle's pocket.

Before Peter knew what was happening, Prince Harry leaped onto the floor. He scooted across the lush carpet and sprang onto Mr. Trifle's bright-blue sneakers before disappearing up the hem of his pants.

"Prince Harry!" Peter cried.

"What?!" Mr. Trifle jiggled and jogged on the spot, not sure why he had the sudden sensation of something crawling up his leg. He tried to shake it out, but the *something* only crawled higher. "Aaah!"

"Dad?" Holly tried to help, but he was flailing his arms and wobbling his hips.

"What's wrong with you?" Mrs. Trifle took a wary step back.

Mr. Trifle twirled like a dog chasing his tail. He wriggled and shook, but nothing helped. "There's something…a *creature*… I can feel it… It might be a spider or a snake…" he realized with horror. "It might be poisonous."

Mr. Trifle did the only thing he thought would save him, something Holly was sure she would never fully recover from.

He undid the zipper on his trousers, dropped his pants, and tossed them aside as if they were infested with spiders.

The entire lobby stared aghast as he stood in his underpants, patting down his legs, trying to find the culprit, which now seemed to be inside his shirt. He was twisting and turning, spinning around frantically, desperate to rid himself of this beast, when he bumped headfirst into a marble pillar.

He stopped and clutched his forehead, dazed and confused.

Mrs. Trifle ran to his aid. "Terry! Are you hurt? Should we call an ambulance?"

That's when Mrs. Trifle spotted the beady eyes of a bright-yellow lizard perched on her husband's shoulder, chewing happily on a piece of Beaut Butts and Guts Protein-Packed Jerky, only inches from her face.

Her scream rose into the ceiling and echoed through the hotel. She turned to run, but her shoe caught on the carpet, and she fell to the floor with a great arm-waving *thud*!

"My ankle!" Mrs. Trifle clutched her leg. "I think I've broken my ankle."

Prince Harry vaulted from Mr. Trifle's shirt onto the floor and dashed back to Peter, who quickly scooped him up.

Mr. Trifle, still a little discombobulated, made a shaky attempt to kneel beside his wife. "Darling? Are you OK?"

"No!" she shrieked. "I most certainly am *not* OK."

Peter inspected his lizard to make sure he wasn't injured by all that jolting and twisting.

Mrs. Trifle spotted them both. "*You!*" She shot Peter a deadly stare. "You brought *vermin* to a spelling bee?"

"He's not vermin," Peter explained. "He's a crested gecko, and he—"

"I don't care *what* he is." Mrs. Trifle pushed herself to sit up. "He's a menace! And he could be diseased, or carrying germs, or—"

"Not Prince Harry," Peter interrupted. "Crested geckos are very clean."

The hotel staff appeared by Mrs. Trifle's side and lifted her carefully into a wheelchair.

"Take me to my room," she ordered before shooting one last look of disdain at Peter.

"I'm so sorry." Peter tried to follow her. "Prince Harry didn't mean it. He's normally very calm, but beef jerky is his favorite."

"Stay away from me," Mrs. Trifle snarled over her shoulder as she was wheeled away.

Mr. Trifle's vision was still a little blurry from the blow to his head. He fished around the floor for his pants and followed after his wife.

"I'm sorry," Peter said to Holly.

"It's not your fault." She offered a weak smile. "The jerky is pretty popular."

"Molly!" Mrs. Trifle bellowed from the open elevator door, a bitter scowl seared across her lips.

"I better go." Holly ran toward her mother and slipped inside the elevator just before the doors slid shut.

~~~~~

After the hotel staff had gently lifted Mrs. Trifle onto the couch and the in-house nurse had treated her ankle, giving Mr. Trifle an ice pack for his forehead, the Trifles were left to themselves.

Mrs. Trifle was in a fit of high dudgeon, madder than Holly had ever seen. Her ankle was bandaged, but despite the nurse confirming it was not broken, Mrs. Trifle insisted she was in utter agony.

"Who brings a rodent to a spelling bee?"

"It's not a rodent," Holly corrected her. "It's a crested gecko."

"I don't care what it is! It could have killed me."

Mr. Trifle held the ice pack against his head with one hand and lightly touched his daughter's arm with the other. He'd seen his wife in this state before, and he knew it'd be better for all of them if they stayed quiet and let her have her say.

"And the boy didn't even apologize."

"He did," Holly insisted. "Maybe you couldn't hear him over your screaming."

Holly didn't mean to sound disrespectful, but the look on her mother's face told her otherwise.

"I *beg* your *pardon*."

Holly shrank. "Peter is a nice person."

"Who keeps deadly vermin in his pockets."

"That's not true," Holly said more loudly than she'd intended.

Mrs. Trifle fixed her daughter with a determined look. "You are not to go anywhere near that boy again."

Holly couldn't help herself; she had to say something. Peter was one of the kindest people she'd ever met. "But he's my friend."

"Not anymore. Not after what he did to me. And your father," she added, almost as an afterthought. She snapped the blanket up to her chin. "Besides," and it was here her mother said something that was truly mean, "you might catch what he has."

Holly's back straightened. "What might I catch?"

"You know." Her mother waved her hand as if it were perfectly obvious.

Mr. Trifle again reached for his daughter's arm in warning, but she stepped out of his grasp. "No, Mother, I don't know."

Mrs. Trifle sighed, exasperated. She whispered as if she were worried she may catch the very same thing if she said it too loudly: "*Being overweight.*"

There were many times in Holly's life when her mother's words left her speechless. This time, however, Holly knew exactly what to say. "How people look has nothing to do with who they are inside."

Mrs. Trifle recognized Nanna Flo's words. "So you'll listen to that old battle-ax but not to your own mother?"

"Nanna Flo happens to be a very wise person."

"I'm your mother, and I'm only trying to protect you."

"No, you're not!" Holly could feel a rage inside her that she had never felt before. "You've never cared one bit about me from the moment you brought me home from the hospital."

In all Mrs. Trifle's life, her daughter had never, not once, disagreed with her, and yet here she was, doing just that.

Mrs. Trifle's cheeks drew in, her lips pursed, and her eyes hardened like two black marbles. "I've worked my whole life to give you what you have, and *this* is the thanks I get. I'm lying here, my leg broken, and you have the nerve to break my heart as well." Her mother began to whimper. "Terry!" she cried. "Tell her to stop being so cruel."

Mrs. Trifle turned back to her daughter with actual fake tears in her eyes.

Holly felt her whole body wither under her mother's gaze. She knew what was going to happen, what *always* happened. To keep the peace, her father would say her mother was right and how Holly should be more respectful. And Holly would half-listen, her mind wandering to what her real family was doing...

But that wasn't what happened at all.

"Holly's right." Mr. Trifle took the ice pack from his bruised head.

Holly spun around and stared at her father, wondering if she'd wanted so badly for him to take her side for once that she'd made it up. But the look on Mrs. Trifle's face told Holly it really did happen.

"What?" Mrs. Trifle's bright-red lipstick sneer made her look like a spooky, deranged clown.

"I said, 'Holly's right,'" he repeated with more confidence. "Nanna Flo's right too. Being overweight isn't contagious, and Peter is a nice boy. If you ask me, Holly is very lucky to have him as her friend."

Mrs. Trifle eyed them both; she wasn't about to give up. "Now you listen here—"

"No," Mr. Trifle interrupted, which shocked him almost as much as it did Mrs. Trifle, who stared at him openmouthed. "I've had enough of listening. The grand final of the Most Marvelous International Spelling Bee is tomorrow, thanks to Holly and her friends, and I am going to be there for my daughter, who has a good chance of winning, which you'd know if you'd bothered to show up for the first round."

Mrs. Trifle flung her hands in the air in frustration. "So now I'm a bad parent?"

"No," Mr. Trifle said carefully. "I think we've been focused on the wrong things, when our daughter is a real champion."

Mrs. Trifle's jaw hardened. "Providing for our family is focusing on the wrong thing?"

"That's not what I—"

"I've flown to London, taken time away from the business, and been separated from *my* children, all for some spelling thingy, and yet I'm the one focused on the wrong things?"

It didn't seem to occur to her that she hadn't been separated from all her children.

"That's not what I meant." No matter how hard Mr. Trifle tried to explain himself, Mrs. Trifle always made him sound so wrong.

"If that's the case, then I'm wasting my time being here." She reached for the phone on the table beside her. "Operator. Send a bellboy to my room, and order me a taxi."

"You're going?" Holly asked. Even though her mother hadn't been very nice and was even at times quite mean, she didn't want her to leave.

Mrs. Trifle stood from the couch, her foot suddenly not so broken, and limped to her room. "I know when I'm not wanted."

~~~~~

Outside the hotel, Mr. Trifle and Holly stood by the taxi as Mrs. Trifle was helped inside.

"Please stay," Holly quietly pleaded.

Mrs. Trifle stared straight ahead. The only thing she said was "Let's go, driver." The car pulled away from the hotel.

Holly felt the sting of watching her mother leave, realizing how much she wanted her to be there, until her dad slipped his hand into hers.

"We'll do this together, eh? You and I."

But Holly couldn't answer. It was the best thing anyone had ever said to her.

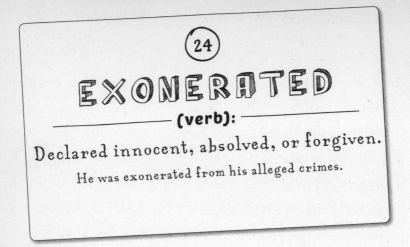

24

EXONERATED

(verb):

Declared innocent, absolved, or forgiven.

He was exonerated from his alleged crimes.

"MR. ELWOOD O'MALLEY, I OFFICIALLY reinstate you as the Queen's representative for the Most Marvelous International Spelling Bee."

In a small room of the Royal Windsor Hotel, a private ceremony was taking place. A woman with gray curls and wearing a trench coat offered Mr. O'Malley her hand.

"Thank you, Your Majesty. It is with great delight and humility that I accept."

"Oh, thank goodness," the Queen said with a chuckle. "I was so hoping you'd say that."

The Wimples, Kapoors, Erikssons, Summer, Mr. Trifle, and Holly applauded.

Esmerelda Stomp actually cracked a smile. At least that's

what it looked like, but it may have been indigestion. "Welcome back, Mr. O'Malley."

"Thank you, Ms. Stomp."

"Harrington Hathaway has been stripped of his awards for his dishonest ways," the Queen continued, "and for potentially damaging the fine reputation of the spelling bee. He has been handed over to the police for questioning." The Queen stepped forward, holding Mr. O'Malley's gaze—even in a trench coat, she wore her royal poise with panache. "But most importantly, Mr. O'Malley, you are officially exonerated of all alleged past indiscretions."

"Thank you, ma'am." Mr. O'Malley could barely speak, his words choked up with emotion. "That means the world to me." Mr. O'Malley pulled his hanky from his pocket and dabbed his eyes.

Summer leaned into India and whispered, "Is he crying again?"

India couldn't answer, because she was crying too. Summer looked around in surprise to find they were all crying.

"I'm awfully sorry about removing you from your position." The Queen winced slightly. "I'm afraid I had no choice when the safety of the children was at risk." She scowled. "I did smell a rat though, which, thanks to these children, was rooted out into the open."

"May I be so bold as to ask?" Mr. O'Malley began. "Harrington was a three-time world spelling champion. Why did you hire me instead?"

The Queen thought for a moment. "I have met many people over the years, Mr. O'Malley, and quite a few of them say what they *think* a Queen wants to hear, but you are genuine. I knew about the accusations of cheating, of course, but I had a hunch there was something fishy about them. I also hold dear to what my beloved papa, the King, taught me about how everyone deserves a second chance. Plus, that Harrington is all hat and no horse."

Mr. O'Malley frowned. "Sorry, ma'am?"

"It's an expression meaning somebody who has accomplished less than appearances would have you believe, so they acquire something that makes them *appear* successful. Back in the Wild West, that could have been a big hat. Whereas you, Mr. O'Malley, are a true and honest person, whom I am lucky to call my friend."

The Queen, against all queenly rules and regulations, reached out and gave Mr. O'Malley a hug.

It took all of Mr. O'Malley's strength not to squeal with glee. As he hugged Her Majesty, the children gave him a unanimous thumbs-up.

"Now for you children, I have something special."

Two royal staff members in disguise, who'd been standing at attention by the door, stepped forward, looking very un-royal in their jeans, flannel shirts, and baseball caps. One held a small velvet-lined wooden box while the other opened the lid and retrieved brass medals strung with royal-blue ribbon.

The Queen hung them around the neck of each speller. "I am awarding you all the Royal Medal of Honor for your work in defending and upholding goodness and decency within the community." She placed the last of the medals around Peter's neck. "And for dealing so expertly with a thorough bully."

Peter stared at the medal. It sparkled in his fingers. He caught a glimpse of Grandpop Eriksson's tearstained face. He was standing beside Nanna Flo, who was just as teary and offered him a tissue from her purse.

"Your Majesty." Dad nervously stepped forward and offered an awkward bow. "Would you mind if I took a photo and wrote an article about what has happened?"

"I would like that *immensely*. That way,

the whole world can read about these intrepid children and my loyal friend, Mr. Elwood O'Malley."

The Queen, Mr. O'Malley, and the spellers posed with broad, beaming smiles.

"I better be off." The Queen took a mustache from her pocket, pressed it above her lips, and donned a Sherlock Holmes–style cap.

"Nice disguise, Your Majesty," Boo said.

"It's one of my favorites."

"You have more than one?"

"Of course. There have been many occasions when I've needed to be *incognito*." She winked. "Good luck for the grand final, everyone. I will be at home watching with my feet up, wishing all of you the very best."

Two royal staffers checked that the corridor was clear before standing aside and bowing as the Queen slipped away.

~~~~

It was fair to say that India didn't sleep much that night. Not after everything that had happened.

Dad also didn't get much sleep. Mr. O'Malley loaned him his computer so he could work on the story. India had told him the whole saga of uncovering Harrington's *underhanded, unscrupulous*, and *conniving* behavior.

Dad was typing well into the next morning while the rest of the Wimples had breakfast and were carrying out some last-minute spelling practice, huddling close and speaking in hushed tones so he could work.

Mom whispered, "Ingenious India, Brave Boo, and their friends foiled a plan so *dastardly*…"

"D-a-s-t-a-r-d-l-y," India whispered back.

"…that even the most *conscientious*…"

"C-o-n-s-c-i-e-n-t-i-o-u-s."

"…of the Queen's staff could not see them *apprehended*."

"A-p-p-r-e-h-e-n-d-e-d."

"It took wit, bravery, and unflinching *audaciousness*…"

"A-u-d-a-c-i-o-u-s-n-e-s-s."

"…to even *contemplate*."

"C-o-n-t-e-m-p-l-a-t-e."

"But she did it," Mom concluded. "Ingenious India proved braver than she ever thought she could be. She was simply *extraordinary*."

"E-x-t-r-a-o-r-d-i-n-a-r-y."

Boo threw his hands in the air and whispered, "Another perfect score!"

"Of course," Nanna Flo said softly. "What else did you expect?"

"I mean it, you know." Mom cradled India's cheeks in her hands. "You're as brave as any person I know."

"Don't forget *ingenious*," Boo pointed out. "You uncovered a mystery that had been unsolved for decades."

"And that no-good snake in the grass Harrington finally got what was coming to him." Nanna Flo rolled up her sleeves. "If I had my way, I'd dunk him in—"

The bedroom door flew open. "It's finished!" Dad's eyes were wide, and his hair stuck out in all directions. "Would you like to read it?"

"Yes, please." India pushed away her breakfast things, and Dad gingerly placed the laptop on the table. As she read the story aloud, Nanna Flo, Boo, and Mom hung on every word, while Dad paced nervously in the background.

It had everything India wanted in a story: vivid details, clever twists, and interesting characters with big hearts, and it kept her fascinated till the very end.

When she finished, no one spoke. Dad stopped pacing and shoved his hands through his hair, which explained why it looked so wild. "What do you think? Is it good enough to be published?"

"It's brilliant!" India hugged her clever, disheveled dad.

"It is?"

"It's one of your best," Boo said.

"I love it," Mom insisted.

"Anyone who doesn't want to publish this needs a new brain." Nanna Flo slammed the table with her palms. "'Cause the one they've got obviously isn't working."

"Thanks, everyone," Dad said, relieved. "O'Malley has sent me the details of the major news sites in the UK, so all I need to do is press 'send' and cross our fingers."

Mom sprang to her feet. "Wimples, it's time for showers and sprucing up so we can escort India to her moment of triumph!"

～～～

The Heritage Ballroom of the Royal Windsor Hotel was abuzz with nervous parents and spellers. Some were giving last-minute tips while others were offering all sorts of rewards if their child won—ponies, cruises, even a ride in a spaceship.

The Wimples stood in the middle of it all with their red scarves snug around their necks.

"How do you feel?" Dad wore a special baby-blue suit and purple bow tie that their neighbor Mrs. Webster had given him for building an enclosed pen for her pig, Wilbur. She threw in a bright-orange shirt that really completed the look.

"I feel fine," India said, and she meant it. The old India would have felt anxious at just the *idea* of standing on an international stage in front of the whole world, but tonight, she wasn't only ready, she couldn't wait for it to start.

"Have you got your lucky hanky?" Nanna Flo asked.

India tapped her pocket. "Right here."

She was wearing her white chiffon dress with three pearl buttons down the front, with the pocket made especially for Nanna Flo's lucky hanky.

"Not that you need it." Nanna waved a hand dismissively. "You're as smart as a whip, or you can dip me in porridge."

"Good luck hug?" Boo asked.

"Yes, please."

As Boo squeezed her tight, he said, "You'll be great, Sis. I know it."

"We'll be here if you need us." Dad tugged at his bow tie as if it were suddenly too tight.

"Not that you will." Mom flashed a broad, confident smile. "Not our *Ingenious India*."

Mom and Dad swooped in for a final hug before making their way to their seats. India stood back and let the excitement of the ballroom swirl around her. The lights sparkled, the cameras were ready—this was it. The Most Marvelous International Spelling Bee Grand Final was about to begin.

She searched the room for her friends and spotted Mr. and Mrs. Kapoor with Rajish.

"It's important not to panic," Mr. Kapoor said, his voice quivering with panic.

"And think of your father," Mrs. Kapoor said, taking her husband's hand, "who will be panicking enough for all of us."

"I find taking a deep breath helps," Rajish told his dad.

Mr. Kapoor took a deep breath. It helped a little. "Thank you, Son."

Mrs. Kapoor wrapped her son in the perfumed swirling folds of her sari. "Win or lose, we are proud of you."

"Extremely proud." Mr. Kapoor held a finger in the air. "I am only speaking the truth!"

Mr. Kapoor couldn't hold back and gave his son another hug. Rajish worried his dad wasn't going to let go, until his mom gently drew his arms away. "He needs to go."

"Of course. Good luck, Son."

As they made their way into the audience to join a waving Mr. Wimple, Rajish joined India.

"Got away?" India raised an eyebrow.

"Just barely. I wasn't sure I'd make it."

India looked up at the stage. Against the backdrop of rich, red theatre curtains, Fozdrake's podium was in place along with neat rows of chairs that were beginning to fill with jittery spellers. "All set, Rajish Kapoor?"

"Ready when you are, India Wimple."

As they climbed the stairs to the stage, in the audience below, a man with slicked-back hair in an elegant suit stood alongside an elegant woman in a long silk gown. The woman was clasping a diamond and ruby bracelet around a young girl's wrist.

"I love it!" Summer held her hand up. The refracted light from the jewels sparkled on her face. "Thank you for coming."

"We wouldn't have missed it." Her mother kissed Summer on both cheeks.

Both parents hugged their daughter one last time before they, too, moved into the stands. Summer threw her head back and climbed the stage stairs like an actress about to receive a major award.

"Your parents came," India said as Summer sat beside her.

"They canceled a very important meeting to be here, and after this, we're going skiing in Austria."

Summer was trying to be all grace and poise when, in a very un-Summer-like way, she squealed.

"Was it about a case?" Rajish asked conspiratorially.

"A case?" Summer frowned.

"The meeting they canceled. Was it about a case?"

"Oh, my parents aren't lawyers. I just said that to make Reko talk."

"But how did you know all that legal stuff?"

"I watch a lot of detective shows." She shrugged. "And you may not have noticed, but I am exceptionally smart."

Rajish sat back and laughed. "And modest."

"Of course," Summer said with a boastful smile.

Not far away, another nervous parent was saying goodbye and good luck to his child.

"I've messed up quite a lot, haven't I?" Mr. Trifle said.

"What do you mean?" Holly asked.

"This spelling bee is a really big deal for you, and I never realized it."

"It doesn't matter." Holly shook her head and frowned.

"It *does* matter. I've been so busy focusing on building the business when I should have been focusing on you." He sighed. "When I was little, my dad blew most of our money at the racetrack. Every time he placed a bet, he thought, *This is it! I'm going to give my family everything they want.* But each time, he'd lose, and Mom would have to figure out how to feed us and pay the rent. There were times I went to bed so hungry that my stomach ached, and I promised myself that my kids would never feel that pain. I thought that'd make me a great dad, but I haven't been so good, have I?"

"You're here with me now, and I'd say that makes you a great dad," Holly said, and she meant it.

"I promise, from now on, I'll be better—starting with cheering for my daughter so the world can know how brilliant she is."

And there it was—what Holly had been waiting for her whole life. Her dad was proud and thought she was brilliant. It was only now she realized how much she'd wanted to hear it.

"Have fun out there." Holly's dad held her tight. "You're going to be amazing."

Holly nestled in his hug for as long as she could before Mr. Trifle left to join the others in the crowd. She felt braver, stronger, knowing he was on her side, and she skipped up the steps to take her place in the grand final.

Close by, Peter's grandpop held him by the shoulders. "You're about to line up with the best spellers in the world, and you deserve to be here as much as any one of them."

"Thanks, Grandpop." Peter seemed distracted.

"Are you OK?"

"Yep," Peter said, which wasn't quite true. "Thanks for being here, Grandpop."

"I should be the one saying thank you. If you hadn't invited me, I'd be at home doing the crossword and having my life revolve around the morning paper and the evening news. And instead, I'm here, about to watch my grandson take to the world stage. Now, off you go." He nodded toward the stage. "Your friends are waiting for you."

Peter turned to see the others waving him over. A small shiver of happiness ran through his body and helped shake off the worst of his fears. They made space for him as he joined their feverish huddle.

"This is it, musketeers," Holly said, toying with the ends of her braids. "The big moment has finally arrived."

"Thanks to a lot of cleverness from us," Summer reminded her.

"There's that humility again," Rajish joked.

"Just saying it like it is." Summer shrugged.

They all laughed except for Peter, who stared into the distance, his hands again clenched in his lap.

"Are you OK?" Holly asked.

It took Peter a few moments before he said, "My dad's not coming back, is he? Even if he does watch the show, there's no guarantee he'll want to actually see me. He hasn't so far, so why would that change now?"

Peter looked so small, and it was all because of this man, his father, who never took the time to know him. Holly, for one, wasn't going to stand for it.

"I don't know what your dad might do, but here's what I *do* know, Peter Eriksson." Holly could feel herself getting fired up for the second time that day. "You're a good person and a good friend, and you're every bit worth coming back for."

"And if your father doesn't realize that," Summer argued, "maybe he doesn't deserve *you*."

"Not only that," Rajish added. "You stood up to Harrington Hathaway!"

"And in the last few days," India said, "you've made four new friends who like you exactly how you are."

Holly hadn't quite finished. "When that music starts and this show begins, I want you to hold your head high and spell like you've never spelled before."

Peter couldn't help but smile. "You're pretty feisty when you get fired up."

"I'm learning." Holly held out her hand. "All for one?"

The others piled their hands on hers. "And one for all."

"OK," Peter decided. "Let's do this."

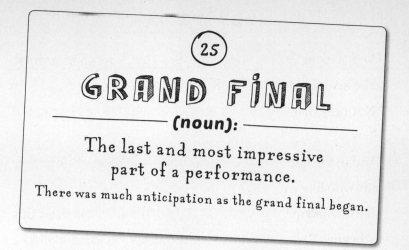

25

GRAND FINAL

—— (noun): ——

The last and most impressive
part of a performance.

There was much anticipation as the grand final began.

"LADIES, GENTLEMEN, AND SPELLERS, WELCOME to the fiftieth anniversary grand final of the Most Marvelous International Spelling Bee."

The music swelled, and the audience was swept into frenzied applause.

Fozdrake Magnifico enjoyed every adoring moment. Dazzling in a red suit with sequined lightbulbs and wearing bright-yellow shoes, his shiny black hair swirled above his head like a scoop of licorice ice cream.

Offstage, in the shadows, stood Mr. O'Malley and Ms. Esmerelda Stomp.

Mr. O'Malley was a portrait of blissful glee. Esmerelda was not, but she did look slightly less miserable than usual.

"Tonight," Fozdrake announced, "you will observe a spine-tingling struggle between sensational spellers. There will be times of tremendous tension, seconds of supreme suspense, but by the culmination of this competition, we will welcome the world's most wondrous wordsmith! Please, join me in welcoming our finalists!"

Lights flooded the stage, revealing two rows of nervous spellers.

As the audience burst into a hearty welcome of cheers, Rajish leaned over. "Good luck, India Wimple."

"You too, Rajish Kapoor."

Fozdrake continued. "In only a matter of hours, one of you will be our winner. One of you will  wonder what to do with a whopping ten thousand dollars." Fozdrake paused, building the tension as he so expertly knew how to do. "And one of you will have the honor of owning this!"

A large spotlight beamed onto the stage and, apart from the slight dent in its side, the Most Marvelous International

Spelling Bee trophy sparkled in all its glory under the waterfall of light.

This *really* sent the audience into a frenzy.

Peter found it almost impossible to steady his heart. The trophy was so close, he could almost touch it. For one small moment, he imagined holding it. He imagined standing in the spotlight, confetti falling, his friends cheering. For a moment, he let himself dare to think he could win.

"As you'll be aware, this is a knockout competition, so if a word is spelled incorrectly, the competitor must leave the stage. The words will be easier at first but will become decidedly more difficult." He paused the famous Fozdrake pause. "By the end of tonight, we shall have our winning wordsmith."

The sequined lights on his suit sparkled almost as much as his scintillating smile.

"Spellers." His voice had the effect of a drumroll. "*Are... you...ready?*"

"Yes...we...are!" The children cried out in unison.

Fozdrake flung his arms into the air in a magnificent swoosh. "Then let the spelling bee...begin!"

Theme music and applause filled the room as all around the world—from a small home in Wormwood, England, to the Queen's private chambers and a packed community hall in a small town called Yungabilla—people tuned in to see who would be the next champion.

Fozdrake held the cards in front of him and, when the noise faded to perfect silence, he began.

"Our first contestant is…Peter Eriksson."

Peter felt as if he'd been punched hard in the chest. It was a feeling he'd had so many times when he was with Bruiser or the other kids at school, and it left him breathless. He gripped the seat so hard that this time, Holly thought he might not get up.

"You have to leave the chair here," she smiled, "or Esmerelda will be furious."

Peter looked at her and released his grip.

"Go get 'em, Peter Eriksson." She held her fists in front of her.

"Thanks, Holly."

Prince Harry wriggled in his jacket pocket, making sure Peter knew he was there for him too.

The lights flooded the stage as Peter stepped to the microphone.

Was his dad watching? Would he recognize him? He wanted more than anything not to be a—

"*Disappointment*," Fozdrake pronounced. "This is a noun meaning the emotion felt when one's expectations are not met."

Peter's shoulders fell, threatening to drag his whole body to the floor.

That's what I am, he thought. *One big disappointment. That's why Dad never bothered to find me.*

Time passed.

"Fifteen seconds remaining."

Fifteen seconds, and he hadn't even started spelling. Peter could see the word. He knew how to spell it.

But he couldn't move. Or speak.

There were only seconds left. Peter had to spell now, or he would be asked to leave the stage.

"Ten seconds remaining."

Still nothing.

A single cheer rose from the audience. It was Grandpop Eriksson. "Go, Peter!"

Peter stared into the blackness and began.

"Disappointment," he said quickly. "D-i-s-a-p-p-o-i-n-t-m-e-n-t. Disappointment."

Fozdrake's eyes lit up in relief. "That is correct!"

The audience applauded. Peter could hear Grandpop cry out, "That's my grandson!"

He turned to see his friends clapping madly and felt a rush through his body like an electric charge.

"I knew you'd do it." Holly nudged him.

Prince Harry wriggled in his pocket again. Peter held open his jacket a smidge and saw the gecko poke out his tongue.

"Prince Harry agrees," Holly whispered.

Fozdrake was in his element, standing in the spotlight. He called more names and pronounced more words.

Anticipation.

Excitement.

Expectation.

"Our next speller is India Wimple."

India stepped to the microphone. She tried to take long, slow breaths to calm herself down. It didn't really work very well.

But she was ready.

"Your word is *audacious*. This is an adjective meaning bold, daring, or adventurous."

It was in Mom's story. India could instantly see it in her mind. "Audacious. A-u-d-a-c-i-o-u-s. Audacious."

The audience applauded, and Nanna Flo cried from the back, "Go, India!" This was followed by a very faint but audible pair of giggles.

Holly was next. Fozdrake held out her card.

Please, please, please, Holly silently pleaded to know the word.

"Your word is *camaraderie*. This is a noun meaning mutual trust and friendship."

Holly took her time to think. It could be *com* or *cam*, but she was almost sure it was *cam*, but what came next? *E* or *a*? Was it *cameraderie* or *camaraderie* or even *cameradery*? She saw the words form and reform in her head, and they all looked correct, until finally, she could see it. She knew it was right.

"Camaraderie," she began with confidence. "C-a-m-a-r-a-d-e-r-i-e. Camaraderie."

"And you are correct!" Fozdrake cried to frantic applause.

Holly skipped to her chair and the company of her widely grinning friends.

Buoyant.

Jauntiness.

Ebullience.

Then came the first of the words to be misspelled. Downhearted spellers shuffled from the stage.

Crestfallen.

Despondent.

Dismayed.

"I would like to call..." Fozdrake prolonged the nervous moment. "Rajish Kapoor."

The room fell deathly silent as he walked across the stage under the hot glare of the stage lights.

"Your word is…" Fozdrake paused. "…*somersault*. This can be a verb or a noun describing an acrobatic movement to turn one's head over one's heels."

Rajish thought carefully. "Somersault. S-o-m…"

He stopped. India silently spelled the rest of the word. *Come on*, she thought. *Spell it with me.*

Rajish frowned. "…e-r-s…"

Holly crossed her fingers.

Peter closed his eyes.

Summer held her breath.

"…a-l-t."

India gasped.

Rajish knew instantly.

"That is, I'm sad to say, incorrect," Fozdrake said with a hint of melancholy.

The audience clapped, and as Rajish left the stage, he sent a quick wink to the others.

India tried not to cry as she watched him go.

The words became harder.

More spellers left the stage. Some reluctantly…

"I won't go! I knew that word! It's not fair." It took both

parents to escort a tall girl with a sharp bob and an even sharper tongue from the stage. Another speller simply sat beside the microphone stand, arms crossed, refusing to move until a furious Esmerelda motioned for security guards, who chased him into the wings.

The numbers of spellers shrank.

Chairs emptied.

Summer was next. She had already spelled *connoisseur* and *miscellaneous* without a thought. She stood at the microphone, smiling for the camera.

"Summer, your word is *palatial*. This is an adjective meaning luxuriously grand or large."

Summer gave her hair a small shake. "Palatial. P-a-l-a-c-i-a-l."

She smiled, unaware of her very small mistake. One letter— that's all it took.

"I'm so sorry," Fozdrake said, "but that is incorrect."

It was only then that Summer realized. "It's a *t*, isn't it?"

Fozdrake nodded. "I'm afraid so, but colossal congratulations on your capacious cleverness."

Summer knew so many words. Hard words that were almost impossible for most adults to spell, but sometimes the easier words tripped a speller up.

India saw Summer purse her lips, for just a moment, as if she were trying to stop herself from crying. She glanced over her shoulder at her friends with a look that seemed to say *over to you* before offering one last smile for the cameras and striding from the stage to emphatic applause.

Formidable.

Grueling.

Toilsome.

They had been spelling for over three hours. There had been tears, tantrums, and trepidation. Now there were only four spellers left.

A young boy called Melville was next. He wore a bow tie beneath a face that was contorted with worry. He was tall and gangly and wore shorts that stopped at his knobby knees. It looked as if they were about to give way any minute. He stumbled as he crossed the stage, which caused him to falter and accidentally knock his glasses to the floor. They fell with a sharp crack and slid across the stage before Peter jumped from his seat and helped him find them.

"Thank you," Melville muttered before putting them back on, only now they had a slight bend to them and sat crookedly on his nose.

"Are you OK to continue?"

Melville nodded. "Yes, Mr. Magnifico."

Fozdrake carefully pronounced the next word. "*Overwrought.* This is an adjective meaning to be extremely or excessively excited or agitated."

Melville held out his hands. They were shaking. With one finger, he wrote out the word on his palm. He shook his hand, as if erasing the letters, and started again, frowning. The audience waited, feeling a little overwrought themselves.

"Over…overwrought," he stammered. "O-v-e-r…" He scribbled on his palm again.

"Fifteen seconds left," Fozdrake said.

Melville's head snapped up in a panic. "r-a-u-g-h-t. Overwrought?" He looked at Fozdrake hopefully.

"I'm afraid that is incorrect, but well done on how you've exceled enormously at this endeavor."

The audience applauded Melville as he shuffled off the stage.

"Ladies and gentlemen," Fozdrake said, gleaming at the audience. "We have our top three!"

Holly, Peter, and India shared an excited laugh. They couldn't quite believe they were there. They heard Nanna Flo, Grandpop Eriksson, *and* Mr. Trifle all cry out.

"I don't care what happens now," Peter decided.

"Me too," India said with the realization. "We made it to the top three."

Holly held out her hand. "All for one?"

"And one for all."

Fozdrake waited for the cheering to die down before he pronounced the next words.

Peter spelled *trailblazing* and *aficionado*. Holly carefully articulated *unyielding* and *accomplishment*, while India expertly handled *virtuoso* before it was her turn again.

"India Wimple," Fozdrake said, "your word is *apotheosis*. This is a noun meaning high point or crowning moment."

This time, India wasn't so clear. The letters formed in her mind, then reformed again in a different order, but she still wasn't sure. She wrote it on her hand. One way, then another.

"Fifteen seconds remaining, India," Fozdrake said.

Holly and Peter crossed their fingers.

"Apotheosis." India knew she didn't have long before she needed to make a decision. "A-p-o…"

The letters reformed again in her mind.

"…t-h-e…"

She tried one last time on her hand.

She decided.

"…s-i-s."

"That is…" Fozdrake tried to hide his disappointment. "Incorrect."

There was a terrible silence. The audience stayed deathly still. India simply smiled.

She'd done it. She'd made it all the way from a small town in Australia to the grand final of the Most Marvelous Spelling Bee in London.

Something she never thought was possible.

"Ladies, gentlemen, and spelling enthusiasts," Fozdrake declared with gusto, "please congratulate India Wimple for being one of the top three spellers of the world!"

The audience sprang to their feet with hoots, whistles, and applause. India left the stage with a small wave as she spotted the rest of the Wimples in their red knitted scarves, jumping and shouting her name. At that same moment, in a small hall in Yungabilla, the same scene was unfolding—including a cheering Daryl in his own red scarf.

"We are down to our final two spellers," Fozdrake announced solemnly. "Holly, your word is *irrepressible*. This is an adjective meaning unstoppable or enduring."

Holly thought carefully. This was a tricky word, which had double letters, but were there two doubles or one? She closed her eyes to see the word more clearly. There were two doubles. She knew it. But was it *ible* or *able*?

There comes a time in every speller's life when they just have to decide, when they settle on the spelling of a word and confidently jump in.

For Holly, that time was now.

"Irrepressible," she said. "I-r-r-e-p-r-e-s-s-a-b-l-e. Irrepressible."

Holly saw the faces of the audience in the front row and knew instantly.

"That is incorrect," Fozdrake said, "which means, if Peter spells this next word without fault, he will be the new champion. If he spells it incorrectly, Holly, you have another chance."

Holly stepped aside while Peter stood ready.

"Your word is," Fozdrake said, his face a picture of perfect poise, "*metamorphosis*. This is a noun meaning any complete change or transformation in character, appearance, or circumstances."

Peter reached for the locket around his neck. He felt Prince Harry wriggle in his jacket pocket. He cleared his mind of everything except that word. He broke it into sections, seeing every letter clearly in its place.

At least he hoped.

"Metamorphosis. M-e-t-a-m-o-r-p-h-o-s-i-s." He looked to Fozdrake. "Metamorphosis."

"Peter Eriksson, it is my duty to tell you...that you are correct! You are the Most Marvelous International Spelling Bee champion!"

Music trumpeted throughout the room. Golden confetti shot into the air and swirled onto the stage like a shimmering snowstorm. The audience hollered and cried while Rajish, Summer, and India hugged each other offstage as if they'd won.

Holly threw her arms around Peter, who was clearly dazed. "Did I win?"

"Yes!" She laughed over the shouting and cheers. "You won!"

Fozdrake fought through the shower of confetti and shimmied between the two stars.

When the audience quieted, he continued. "Ladies, gentlemen, word lovers everywhere, what a tremendous tournament of talent from two talented teammates. From this night forth, Peter and Holly, the whole world will know both of you as the intelligent, ingenious, and incomparable young people you are."

From the wings, Mr. O'Malley appeared with a bouquet of flowers. "As a token of our eternal admiration, Holly, please accept these flowers…inside of which you'll find a little something extra."

Holly took an envelope from among the flowers and opened it. Her hand flew to her mouth, and her eyes widened.

"Can you share your prize with the audience?" Fozdrake prompted.

"It is a voucher for Ms. Macy's International Book Bonanza for"—she almost couldn't say it—"one thousand dollars. Thank you!"

Mr. O'Malley led Holly to the side of the stage while Fozdrake gathered the trophy. "Peter Eriksson, congratulations! You are the newest Most Marvelous International Spelling champion."

Fozdrake handed over the trophy. Peter worried he might drop it, he was shaking so much, until Esmerelda guided Grandpop Eriksson to the stage, and they held it together.

"I knew you could do it!" Grandpop had no hope of stopping his tears. "Never doubted for a second."

"And here," Fozdrake said, "is your check for ten thousand dollars! Is there anything you'd like to say?"

"Is this really happening?"

The audience laughed.

"It most certainly is," Fozdrake said.

Peter took a few moments to think. "Firstly, I want to thank my mom, who's watching right now. You're the best mom on the planet. And Grandpop Eriksson, for standing by me when you were going through your own tough times. You're my hero."

Grandpop nodded, unable to say anything for fear of becoming a blubbering mess.

"And thank you to Mr. O'Malley and Ms. Stomp and my newfound spelling friends. And finally," Peter said as he stared straight into the camera, "what I really want to say is this: I'm just a regular kid from a regular house, and if this can happen to me, it can happen to you too."

"Ladies and gentlemen," Fozdrake announced. "The world's newest Most Marvelous International Spelling Bee champion."

The audience were instantly on their feet, cheering and crying out his name.

"Nice one, Peter."

"You deserve it!"

The room was a swirl of music and applause. Peter waved to the crowd and drank it all in. He felt light-headed, as if he were standing on the world's tallest mountain, watching the most magnificent view. Beside him was Grandpop, and in front were the Wimples, the Kapoors, the Beauregard-Champions, Holly, and her dad.

All clapping, just for him.

And he didn't think about Bruiser or his dad.

Not once.

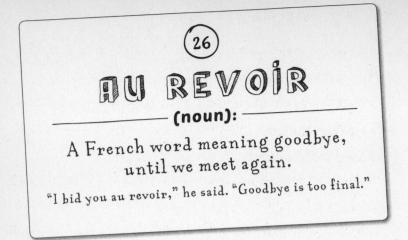

26

AU REVOIR

(noun):

A French word meaning goodbye,
until we meet again.

"I bid you au revoir," he said. "Goodbye is too final."

IT'S ALMOST TIME TO LEAVE the Wimples, but before we do, there were a few last things that happened in London.

After the grand final, the Wimples, Kapoors, Beauregard-Champions, Erikssons, and Trifles went out for a sensational dinner to celebrate, courtesy of the Beauregard-Champions. It was during the meal that Dad's phone started beeping. A lot. His story had gone viral. News organizations all around the world splashed it on their front pages. It was called, "Spelling Sleuths Stop Skullduggery."

And there, on every site, was a photo of the kids, Mr. O'Malley, and the Queen of England.

Mr. Kapoor raised his glass: "To the spelling champions."

Everyone clinked their glasses.

"And to Arnie Wimple, journalist extraordinaire!"

Dad shook his head. "No, I'm not—"

"Oh yes, you are!" Mr. Kapoor raised his pointer finger. "I am only speaking the truth!"

Mom planted a very big kiss on Dad's cheek.

"Now it's your turn to put up with the kissing," Rajish said quietly to India.

Dinner lasted long into the night, with Nanna Flo and Grandpop Eriksson leading duets on the karaoke machine and everyone taking turns holding the trophy and having their picture taken with the champion. Finally, they all stumbled back to their hotel rooms.

Which is when Dad checked his email. There was one from the *Huddersfield Herald*, wanting to interview him for a job.

"What should I say?" His brow was riddled with worry wrinkles.

"Tell them you're a world-class journalist," India said.

"Who is dedicated and smart," Boo added.

"And wanted by news agencies everywhere," Mom reminded them.

"And if they don't give you the job, they must have cow manure between their ears, and I won't mind telling them," Nanna Flo concluded.

"Thank you," Dad said, feeling better.

"When is the interview?" Mom asked.

Dad figured out the time difference, and his face went white. "Now," he gulped.

As if on cue, the phone rang. "It's them."

Mom kissed him again. "You'll be fine."

"Go, Dad!" India said.

Boo nodded. "You've got this."

"The Wimples are on a winning streak!" Nanna Flo rubbed her hands together. "I can feel it."

Dad took the call in the bedroom while the rest of the Wimples waited anxiously in the living room. Boo rested his ear against the door, trying to listen.

"What's he saying?" India asked.

"There are a lot of muffled words…and laughter," Boo whispered. "Or maybe crying. It's hard to tell."

"Let me hear." India put her ear against the door too. "Now there's just silence."

"Shove over." Nanna Flo muscled in as well. "You're right. He's doing a lot of listening. Or maybe it's already over."

"So why hasn't he come out?" Mom squeezed in too.

They were straining to hear what was going on when Dad opened the door and only just managed to stop his entire family from toppling inside. "Whoa! Easy there, everyone."

The Wimples straightened themselves up and huddled like anxious penguins.

"What did they say?" India was trying to read Dad's face but found it impossible.

"They saw my story and liked it. They said I had a good style."

"That means they know what they're talking about." Nanna Flo stabbed at the air.

"What else did they say?" Mom asked.

"They wanted to know if I had any other story ideas, and when I began telling them all, they stopped me midway."

"Talking too much?" Boo asked.

Dad winced. "I was nervous."

"What happened next?" Mom pressed.

"They gave me a job."

"As a journalist?" Nanna Flo asked, breathless.

Dad took a moment to answer. "Yep. I'm going to be a journalist again!"

Boo threw his arms around Dad, followed by India, Mom, and Nanna Flo in their usual ecstatic huddle.

"This calls for another celebration!" Nanna Flo opened her purse and took out a handful of specially wrapped mint chocolates. "I took them from the restaurant."

The Wimples gathered on the couch, eating chocolates, while

Dad talked about the articles he'd like to write and the people he'd interview—and the toilets he wouldn't have to unblock any more or the roofs he wouldn't have to climb to rescue the occasional climbing goat. India listened as she snuggled with her family, which felt as warm and cozy as any place she knew.

The next morning, packed and ready to leave, the Wimples, Kapoors, Beauregard-Champions, Erikssons, and Trifles stood in the lobby of the Royal Windsor Hotel.

Waiting for them was Mr. Elwood O'Malley.

"It has been the utmost pleasure to have met you all," he said. "Not only for your spelling prowess, but for your kindness. If it wasn't for you, the grand final would never have happened, my reputation would be ruined, and I would no longer be the Queen's representative."

"We did what we thought was right." Holly smiled.

"We did what should have been done a long time ago," India added.

"And we did it with style," Summer reminded them.

"And we'd do it again," Rajish said.

Prince Harry poked his nose from his jacket pocket. "All of us," Peter said, patting his scaly friend.

"You have my eternal gratitude," Mr. O'Malley said. "*Au revoir*, as the French say. Until we meet again."

Just before they left, Esmerelda came out to say a final farewell.

She clutched her clipboard against her chest and gave one short, sharp wave. "Goodbye."

India didn't expect a goodbye from the director, not after her declaration of not liking kids or spelling bees, but with only one small glance to the others, they began to walk closer to Esmerelda.

"What are you doing?" She looked around as if she suddenly wanted to escape. "Don't even think about it. I'm warning you…"

But it was too late. All five children flung their arms around her.

"What are you doing?"

"It's called a hug," Holly explained.

"It's what people do when they like each other." India continued hugging Esmerelda, who held her hands in the air as if she were being mugged.

"You should try it sometime," Rajish said. "You might like it."

"That's enough now." Esmerelda stepped away and brushed herself down. "Hugs! *Pah!*"

Even though she looked annoyed, India could tell she didn't mean it.

There was a great kerfuffle of hugs and goodbyes, tears and promises to keep in touch, before the taxi whisked the Wimples to the airport.

It was on the long journey home that the Wimples finally spoke to Mom about Boo going back to school. It took quite a lot of convincing and some dealmaking—there were even tears—but they worked as a team, and Mom eventually agreed.

~~~~~

On his first day of school, the Wimples walked with him to the front entrance.

"You don't all need to be here." Boo looked at the other kids who came to school without being surrounded by their entire family.

"But this is a big day for the Wimple family." Dad drove his hands through his hair so that it stood out in all directions.

"And we want to make sure you're OK," Mom sniffed.

"Even though we know you will be," Nanna Flo said, trying to be strong. "You're a Wimple, and we Wimples never give up! You're going to be just fine."

Kids skated by and rode past on their bikes. "Hey, Boo!"

Boo waved before turning to his family. "Yes, but now it might be time to go." None of them moved. "I have my asthma kit, my teacher has my asthma plan, the school has all your numbers—everything's going to be fine."

Mom wasn't so keen. "Maybe we could walk you to class and see where you're sitting?"

"I'll be OK on my own." Boo sent India a *help me* look.

"We better go," she said. "Don't want to be late on our first day back."

Finally, Mom, Dad, and Nanna Flo waved goodbye.

Boo and India watched them leave.

"Don't get me wrong, I love them and all, but I'm so glad they've left," Boo said.

"Are you sure you'll be OK?" India asked.

"India…" Boo warned.

"OK. I'll stop. It just might take me some time."

"Boo!" A boy with scruffy hair skateboarded by.

"Liam!" Boo tore across the yard.

It took all of India's strength not to chase him and make sure the running wasn't going to bring on an attack. But she'd promised. However, she planned to not be too far away so she could keep a sneaky eye on him. At least at the beginning.

~~~~~

So we leave this story for the last time, a few months later, with the Wimples and Daryl reclining in the sunshine in deckchairs along Main Street in Yungabilla.

They were wearing sunglasses and sitting across from the town's newest addition.

"She's a real beauty!" Nanna Flo shook her head, still not able to believe it.

"It makes quite an impression," Mom agreed.

"And it's so big!" Boo craned his head back to take it all in.

"It's a ripper," Daryl said in awe. "Nothing less than deserved."

"And it's all because of our little girl." Dad beamed.

The object of their admiration was a carved statue called *The Big Dictionary* that had been placed in the very center of town. Below it was a gold plaque, which said:

DEDICATED TO INDIA WIMPLE,
YUNGABILLA'S INTERNATIONAL
SPELLING CHAMPION

India stared at the statue. It was a surreal moment, like she were making it all up.

Ever since its unveiling, people drove from all over the country to have their photo taken next to it. Like Mayor Bob had predicted, it made Yungabilla a tourist destination not to be missed.

The campground was overflowing with vans and tents, Gracie's Café was busier than ever, and Mrs. O'Donnell at the bakery had to wake up even earlier to bake enough muffins, scones, and lamingtons—which she kept in a special glass case in case Bessie came by—but it was her delicious blueberry cheesecakes that people wanted most.

"How does it feel?" Nanna Flo asked. "To have your own statue?"

"And to be an international spelling champion?" Mom added.

"And a world traveler who has hobnobbed with the Queen?" Boo said.

"And super sleuth," Daryl reminded them.

"Can't forget that!" Dad declared.

India thought about it before saying, "That's all very nice, and I liked London, but to tell the truth, I like being home much better."

"I like that too," Daryl said. "Yungabilla's not the same without the Wimples around."

And with that, they all settled back into their deckchairs on Main Street in Yungabilla, where our story of the Wimples first began.

About the Author

Deborah Abela is short and not very brave, which may explain why she writes books about spies, ghosts, soccer legends, and children living in a flooded city battling sea monsters and sneaker waves. When she was in fourth grade, Deb had a wonderful teacher called Miss Gray, who made reading and spelling spectacular fun. Deb has won awards for her books but mostly hopes to be as brave as her characters.

Find out more about what she's been up to at her website, deborahabela.com.

Read where India's adventures began in
The Stupendously Spectacular Spelling Bee!

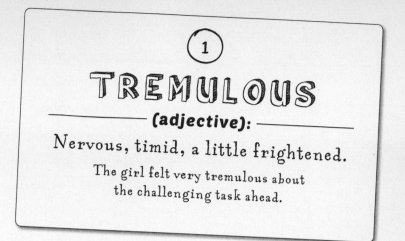

TREMULOUS

(adjective):

Nervous, timid, a little frightened.

The girl felt very tremulous about
the challenging task ahead.

INDIA WIMPLE COULD SPELL. BRILLIANTLY. On Friday nights, she and her family would huddle in front of the TV in their pajamas, in their small house in Yungabilla, and watch the Stupendously Spectacular Spelling Bee.

India adored her family—it was the thing that mattered most to her. There was her younger brother, Boo; Mom; Dad; and Nanna Flo.

Nanna Flo hadn't always lived with them. She'd moved in after she fell and broke her wrist during an especially enthusiastic yoga move. She wasn't happy about leaving the home where she'd lived with Grandpop for over forty years. She made kind of a fuss, mostly by stomping around and saying "Fiddlesticks!" a lot, which was as close to swearing as Nanna Flo ever got. But she soon realized she was much happier surrounded by her family, and the stomping and almost swearing stopped.

One particular Friday night, where our story begins, the Wimples huddled in front of the TV, as they usually did. But this night was different. It was the Stupendously Spectacular Spelling Bee Grand Final and, as it happened, it was also the day the Wimples' lives would change forever.

Boo stretched out on the floor with his chin cupped in his hands, while Mom, Dad, Nanna Flo, and India sat snugly on the sofa. Ernie rested at their feet.

Mom, Dad, and Nanna Flo were people. Ernie was a large statue of a bulldog that Nanna Flo insisted on taking with her everywhere, much to her family's embarrassment. Not only was Ernie remarkably heavy, but he was also incredibly ugly and had the unfortunate habit of scaring young children.

On the TV was a tiny, barely there girl with bouncy, black curls, whose mouth was wide open, as if she'd just had a very big shock. Her name was Katerina. After months of spelling bee heats held all around the country, there were only two spellers left. Katerina was one of them, and her mouth was wide open because her opponent had misspelled his last word. He moved aside with a shake of his head and Katerina stepped up to the microphone.

She looked so small standing on the main stage of the Concert Hall at Sydney Opera House. Dwarfed by its huge, arched ceilings, she took a deep breath, looking more like a girl about to fall off a mountain—a very high mountain—than someone who was simply going to spell.

Her body quivered. Her curls shook. It was indeed a *tremulous* moment.

The camera cut to her parents sitting in the front row. Her dad gave her a thumbs-up and her mother raised crossed fingers.

This seemed to make Katerina relax. A little.

But then she looked like she was on top of that mountain again.

Not far from her, sparkling in the stage lights, was the Stupendously Spectacular Spelling Bee trophy. If she spelled the next word correctly, she would be the new champion and the trophy would be hers.

The Concert Hall fell deathly silent as the pronouncer, Philomena Spright, prepared to reveal the next word. Philomena had been the official pronouncer longer than India had been alive. Philomena's hair sat perched on her head in a perfect soft-serve-ice-cream swirl. She always wore very glamorous dresses and heels so high that India worried she might trip over them one day.

But she never did.

Philomena Spright held a small card with her bright-red fingernails in front of her equally bright-red lips.

On the card was written, quite possibly, the final word of the competition.

Very carefully, Philomena pronounced, "*Tremulous,* an adjective meaning nervous, timid, or a little frightened. Using it in a sentence, I could say, *The girl felt tremulous at facing the next word of the spelling bee grand final.*"

The audience quietly chuckled before settling into an anxious silence.

Katerina took a few seconds to think.

In the Wimple family home, far, far away, India whispered the spelling of the word without hesitation.

"That's the right answer, isn't it?" Boo asked.

India's auburn ponytail swung as she nodded. "I'm sure of it."

Katerina crossed both fingers behind her back and began to spell. "Tremulous. T-r-e-m-u-l-o-u-s." She finished by saying the word with one final, hopeful flourish. "Tremulous?"

Philomena Spright paused for effect, which she always did. It was her way of building suspense, of making the audience and the contestants lean in, eager to hear her verdict. She never revealed the result too early by showing a smile or a frown. She stared at the girl for several excruciatingly long seconds before saying, in her most serious voice, "Katerina, I'm afraid that answer is...*correct!*"

It was only then that Philomena Spright smiled a broad, victorious smile. "You are the new Stupendously Spectacular Spelling Bee champion!"

Katerina's hands flew to her cheeks. The lights flashed, theme music blared, and a shower of confetti sprinkled down from above like a colorful snowfall. The audience was on its feet, cheering and clapping.

"You were right," Boo whispered to his sister. "As always."

Philomena Spright handed Katerina the trophy, which was almost too big for her to hold. Her parents rushed onto the stage, crying and hugging their daughter.

When the applause eventually died down, Philomena Spright spoke into the microphone. "Katerina, tell everyone at home how this moment feels."

Katerina hugged the trophy with both hands and thought for a few seconds before saying, "From the time I was a little girl, I've dreamed of winning the Stupendously Spectacular Spelling Bee." She paused, a small tear forming in the corner of her eye. "And now it's really happening."

More tears flowed as Katerina's mom and dad hugged her tight.

"It most certainly is happening," Philomena Spright declared.

"From thousands of spellers, competing in hundreds of rounds and one riveting grand final, you are our new champion! And now for your prizes." She took an envelope from the trophy stand. "As always, there is a five-hundred-dollar gift card for Mr. Trinket's Book Emporium."

Katerina accepted it with an awestruck "thank you."

"And that's not all. We can now reveal your grand prize."

There was a drum roll.

The Wimple family listened with great anticipation. There was a different grand prize each time. There'd been a family cruise and a trip to the world's tallest toy store in New York. Once it was a vacation to the Wizarding World of Harry Potter.

"You know how you like amusement parks?" Philomena Spright asked.

"Yes." Katerina nodded feverishly.

"You and your family are going to…Disneyland, with five thousand dollars in spending money!"

Katerina squealed. She couldn't help it—it just came out. "Thank you! Thank you! Thank you!"

"You are welcome, welcome, welcome!"

The family fell into hugs and even more joyful tears.

Philomena Spright turned to the camera. "That's it for another Stupendously Spectacular Spelling Bee. I'd like to thank all our *sensational* spellers and our *astounding* audience. Were you able to spell all the words correctly? Would *you* like the chance to stand on this very stage? If you think you have what it takes, why not sign up?"

She looked down the barrel of the camera and, for a moment, India Wimple thought the pronouncer was speaking only to her. "Because our next Stupendously Spectacular Spelling Bee champion could be *you!*"

Philomena Spright didn't move for what felt like several minutes, pointing her shiny, red fingernail at India with the smallest of knowing smiles on her lips.

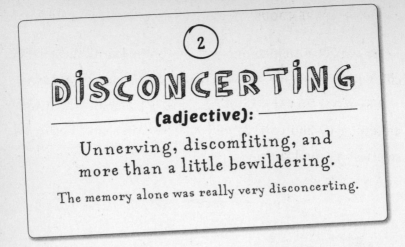

2

DISCONCERTING

(adjective):

Unnerving, discomfiting, and more than a little bewildering.

The memory alone was really very disconcerting.

BOO NUDGED HIS SISTER. "PHILOMENA'S right—it could be you."

India scoffed. "Me?"

"Yes," Mom said. "Why not?"

"Because TV is only for the very rich, the very famous, or the very pretty...and I'm not any of those things."

"I disagree!" Dad argued. "It's true we're not rich or famous, but as for being pretty, you are beautiful from your head down to your toes."

"Thanks, Dad, but I think you might be biased."

"Fiddlesticks!" Nanna Flo blurted. "What a load of codswallop! Your father's right or you can dunk me in a barrel of barbecue sauce!"

"It would be exciting to see you onstage with all those other children," Mom said, "showing the world how clever you are."

"It's true." Boo sprang upright in his pajamas, which were a little baggy and covered with planets and stars. "You're the smartest person I know."

"Do you really think I could?" India asked, sounding a bit tremulous herself.

"We *know* you could!" Dad scooted so far forward on the couch that he almost fell off. "Who do I ask when I don't know how to spell a word?"

"India," Boo answered.

"And who sits there spelling every word correctly every single time?"

"India," Boo repeated.

The TV screen was jammed with people laughing and calling Katerina's name, while photographers elbowed their way closer to take her picture. She was totally surrounded. India felt breathless and light-headed.

She sighed. "And who freezes every time she stands in front of an audience?"

There was a pause. Everyone knew who she meant, but they pretended they didn't.

It was true. India Wimple was terribly, horribly shy, and whenever she found herself the center of attention, her cleverness seemed to disappear.